Why was he r... a beautiful wo... just met?

It was ludicrous! No, it wasn't ludicrous; that was the point. There was nothing in the least bit funny about the situation. He was more than attracted to Miranda Gibbs—he was in danger of falling in love with her.

In love with her!

Nonsense. Impossible! But it wasn't impossible. She'd bowled him over, staggered him with her beauty, made his palms sweat. He, the sophisticated bachelor. He groaned. If she came into the practice and he was to survive he was going to have to play it cool—very cool. . .

Margaret O'Neill started scribbling at four and began nursing at twenty. She contracted TB and, when recovered, did her British Tuberculosis Association nursing training before general training at the Royal Portsmouth Hospital. She married, had two children, and with her late husband she owned and managed several nursing homes. Now retired and living in Sussex, she still has many nursing contacts. Her husband would have been delighted to see her books in print.

Recent titles by the same author:

MORE THAN SKIN-DEEP

A CAUTIOUS LOVING

BY

MARGARET O'NEILL

MILLS & BOON®

All the characters in this book have no existence outside the imagination of the author, and have no relation whatsoever to anyone bearing the same name or names. They are not even distantly inspired by any individual known or unknown to the author, and all the incidents are pure invention.

First published in Great Britain 1997
Harlequin Mills & Boon Limited,
Eton House, 18-24 Paradise Road, Richmond, Surrey TW9 1SR

ISBN 0 263 80189 6

Set in Times 10 on 11 pt. by
Rowland Phototypesetting Limited
Bury St Edmunds, Suffolk

03-9706-55385-D

Printed and bound in Great Britain
by Mackays of Chatham PLC, Chatham

CHAPTER ONE

'AND now tell us, Miss Gibbs,' said Dr Brodie, some twenty minutes into her interview, 'why you want to leave a busy health centre in Birmingham for what, by comparison, might be considered a small, cosy practice in a little cathedral city like Combe Minster? Hardly a career move for an experienced manager, I would have thought.'

Black eyebrows arched high above the rim of his spectacles. 'Do you think it's going to be a doddle before you move on to higher things? If so, forget it. This is a newly created post—we're looking for dedication, solid commitment and hard work, and this is reflected in the salary that we're offering.'

His voice was deep, velvet smooth, but his words were blunt, uncompromising and his manner brusque.

He took off the heavy horn-rimmed glasses and unhurriedly studied the woman seated composedly opposite. Miss Miranda Gibbs, aged thirty. Stunning! Brains as well as beauty. Sea-green, intelligent eyes, glinting with humour, honey-golden hair—with delicate tendrils wisping round her face in little half-curls—coiled elaborately at the nape of her slender neck. A desirable, kissable neck!

He brought his racing thoughts up with a jerk.

What the hell am I thinking about, and why the hell am I being deliberately aggressive towards this gorgeous creature? Because, he answered himself, I feel vulnerable to this woman's beauty and I'm as susceptible as the next man to a beautiful woman and want to resist her.

Susceptible! He glanced at his three male colleagues. They were susceptible, all right. Usually laid-back Bill Jones was all alert, eager; and testy, acerbic Dennis Withers, on the edge of retirement, was looking almost benevolent.

As for Val Thorpe, the merry widower, he was all but drooling but, then, he was a sucker for any halfway attractive woman, let alone a beauty like Miss Gibbs. Even crisp, practical, middle-aged Kay Brent, the one female on the panel, seemed impressed by the bright, lovely Miranda.

OK, Brodie, forget her looks and judge her on merit.

A wizard at handling people, according to her glowing references, coping admirably with a large staff. Well qualified, splendid CV. Registered general nurse, admin and managerial certificates, and plenty of grass-roots experience. Thirty, just right. Best candidate we've had.

She would be an asset to the practice. So—why do I feel so wary about taking her on; feel that it would be a mistake? Am I overreacting to her beauty? And if so, why?

The cathedral clock across the sunlit square chimed a melodious four o'clock. The famous Combe Minster chimes.

Miranda, guessing at some of his tumultuous thoughts and knowing that her fabulous looks were not always an asset, met Thomas Brodie's unreadable dark brown eyes squarely. He had given her quite a grilling.

Since the beginning of her interview he had piled on the pressure and, at times, come very close to being downright rude. But why? Was he naturally aggressive, or was this just an interviewing technique—a tough ploy to frighten off waverers?

Well, she wasn't a waverer; she knew what she wanted and was going all out to get it. And she wanted this job. His very antipathy made her even more determined.

She lifted her finely moulded chin, and said firmly, 'As nurse manager, I would be committed and dedicated. I've never shirked hard work. And I've no ties—no dependants to distract me—I'm unencumbered. I've a sister who is happily married and lives in York, and no other near relatives.'

She paused for a moment. 'And, *no*, Dr Brodie, I do *not* think that working here in Combe Minster would be a doddle. It will be different to working for a conglomerate of doctors in a large health centre, but it will have its own problems—and I'd like to be the one who solves them. And there will be an opportunity here to do some hands-on nursing, which I very much want to do.'

'Hmm,' grunted Brodie, frowning as he replaced his spectacles on his high-bridged nose. He leaned back in his chair, still eyeing her thoughtfully. He liked her directness. He liked the way her extraordinary sea-green eyes met his. If only he could rid himself of the suspicion that she had an ulterior motive for applying for this job. . . If only he were not so conscious of her beauty and saw it as a threat. Unencumbered, she'd said. Did that mean that she was man-free?

There was a moment's silence as Miranda surveyed him as steadily as he surveyed her. Was he convinced? she wondered, or was he one of those men who always doubted a woman's ability to be single-minded about their work? Couldn't tell from his expression. An interesting face—lean, hawkish, good strong jaw, firm mouth. Like his hair—well cut, jet black with a hint of grey above his ears.

The brief silence was broken by Dr Brent who, raising her eyebrows above twinkling, alert eyes, asked the very question that was bothering Brodie. 'What, *no attachments* at all, Miss Gibbs?'

'No attachments,' replied Miranda positively, smiling back at the doctor, who was quite obviously referring to men and asking, obliquely, if there was a current man in the background.

'Good,' said Dr Brent succinctly.

I believe I'll get her vote, thought Miranda, and, with luck, the other three men. But the tough Dr Thomas Brodie—I don't think I've won him round, and he seems to carry a lot of weight.

Dr Brodie closed the file in front of him and looked at his colleagues. 'Anything else?' he asked. There was a negative murmur from the other doctors, who shook their heads and smiled across at Miranda.

Only Dr Brodie didn't smile. He nodded, stood up and strode briskly round the table. Miranda rose to meet him.

'Thank you for coming, Miss Gibbs.' He held out his hand, and she put hers into it. They shook hands formally.

'We'll be in touch tomorrow.' His voice was curt. 'We have to discuss our findings with our colleagues who were not present at the interviews. There are several candidates to consider, but we want to tie this appointment up as soon as possible. I understand that you're staying at The Mitre and we can reach you there.'

'Yes, for a few days. I'm combining business with pleasure and taking a short holiday. I aim to explore this part of the country. I was born in Dorset; lived here as a child.'

'Did you indeed, and is *that* the real reason why you applied for this post—because you want to get back to your roots?' His voice was silky; his eyes gleamed behind his specs.

Miranda held down her anger. The man was infuriating. Why did he persist in undermining the reasons she had given for wanting to join the practice?

'No,' she said evenly. 'I've given you my reasons; the fact that the practice happens to be in Dorset is a bonus. I trained in London and have since worked in other big cities. Now I want to find out what it is like to work in a small urban city with a different range of needs. This is a professional move, first and last. Surely you can accept that, Dr Brodie?'

His eyes searched hers for a moment. Quite suddenly he seemed to make up his mind about something and said, in a thoughtful sort of voice, 'Yes, I can accept that, Miss Gibbs.' A glimmer of a smile touched the corners of his mouth. 'Do enjoy your stay in Combe Minster. We'll be in touch tomorrow, by eleven, to inform you of our decision one way or another.' He inclined his head in a dismissive fashion.

The interview was over. He strode across the room. Miranda shook hands with the other three doctors and followed him to the door.

He held it wide open. 'Goodbye,' he said as she passed through. 'Have a pleasant evening.' And then, to her surprise—perhaps trying to make up for his earlier churlishness—he added, 'If you want a change from The Mitre, I can recommend dinner at The Poet and Pigeon. It's next door to the theatre in Chantry Street.'

'Thank you,' murmured Miranda as she turned and walked away down the corridor toward the stairs. She didn't look back, but felt that he was watching her.

Slowly she made her way across the busy square. There were tea-rooms, she had been told, in the basement of the monks' cloisters in the cathedral.

The cloisters were pleasantly cool and dim, and thronged with summer visitors. The self-service café, with its stone-flagged floor and small barred windows, was even dimmer and busier. She collected tea and, feeling suddenly hungry, a squashy Danish pastry and sat down at a small empty table tucked away in an alcove.

In spite of her outward calm, nervous reaction to the grilling she had received had left her feeling limp. Low blood sugar! She swallowed a mouthful of tea and forked a delicious piece of creamy pastry into her mouth, chewing thoughtfully as she mulled over her interview.

On the whole, it had been a good interview. Each of the doctors had done their share of probing into her professional ability, and she had been exhilarated by it. Sure of her ground, she knew that she had answered their in-depth questions competently and intelligently.

She knew, too, that they'd been impressed by her imaginative grasp of the problems involved in amalgamating three small practices into one. . .even the doubting Dr Brodie.

But the tail end of the interview had been quite sticky.

Miranda sighed as she sipped at her second cup of tea. She hadn't expected Thomas Brodie's suspicious questioning. Why did he find it so difficult to accept that she wanted to widen her experience by working in an entirely different environment? Why did he have to dig, as if he suspected that she had something to hide, when her references and CV told him all he needed to know?

OK, he was right in thinking that she might have tried for a job in the faster lane, offering quicker promotion on a short-term basis.

But she'd made it clear that she didn't want that. She wanted a more secure contract for a few years, something that would offer satisfying administrative experience and the opportunity to do some hands-on nursing—impossible on the higher rungs of the promotional ladder.

The other members of the panel had appreciated that, so why not the difficult Dr Brodie? Only when he learned that she had been born in Dorset had he seemed disposed to believe that she might have sound reasons for wanting to live and work in Combe Minster.

Well, she thought, if I get the job—no, with a sudden rush of confidence, *when* I get the job—I'll have it out with him one day, face to face. Ask him why he was suspicious. Meanwhile, working with him will be a challenge.

And she enjoyed a challenge, found it stimulating. That's what being a career woman was all about, she reflected, and, at this moment in time, being a dedicated professional was all she was interested in.

Certainly this time there would be no entanglements. No having to fight off the unwanted attentions of a senior colleague, who wouldn't take no for an answer. No way would she allow that to happen again. Of course she couldn't stop men being bowled over by her beauty, but that was something she could handle. Had been handling since she was in her teens, without anyone getting seriously hurt. . .until Steven.

Steven, arrogant and handsome and used to getting his own way with women, hoist on his own petard. Helplessly in love with her, he had almost gone to pieces when she had turned him down. She hadn't wanted to hurt him, but she couldn't pretend to a love that she hadn't felt.

'You're a cold, hard, unfeeling woman,' he'd flung at her, 'substituting a career for love. Miranda, I don't think you know what love is.' His words surfaced now as she sat in the cathedral tea-rooms.

Ruthlessly she squashed the accusation. It wasn't true. She was as capable of love as any woman, but love for and with the right man—and until he came along her career was the most important factor in her life.

That's why she wanted this Combe Minster job, which required hands-on nursing *and* management skills. And she liked what she had seen of the small, bustling city—little more than a market town, really, with narrow ancient streets tucked away behind the busy centre.

But, more importantly, she had taken to the doctors she had met that afternoon and had quickly established some sort of rapport with them. And, oddly enough, though he had infuriated her she had liked the hard-hitting Dr Brodie. She liked the lean, intelligent face, high forehead and widow's peak of black hair, the deep-set dark brown eyes, unreadable and enigmatic though they were.

Fortyish, she guessed, not conventionally handsome, but with strong, good features. He had lots of very male charisma, but she felt instinctively that he could be trusted and, as a bonus, was unlikely to be influenced by her beauty but would judge her on merit.

She wondered what he was doing at that moment—perhaps settling her future!

And, on that thought, she left the café to explore and enjoy the rest of the cathedral, which—with its three sturdy towers—dominated the city.

On the other side of the square, on the second floor of the Regency building housing the cathedral practice, the five doctors were winding up their post-mortem on the interviews.

'Well, my money's on Miranda Gibbs,' said Kay Brent. 'She's far and away the best of the bunch—brilliant references and CV, intelligent, authoritative and with a sense of humour. I like that.'

'If we take her on, and I rather think we should, she'll need it.' Dennis Withers spoke with his usual terseness. 'But, then, so will any of the outside candidates. There's bound to be *some* friction with Liz Fuller and her cronies if she doesn't get the job.'

'Yes, having an insider's always a problem. I did warn Liz that because she's our senior practice nurse it wouldn't be automatic, but she wanted to try for it anyway.' Thomas Brodie frowned. 'But her experience is too limited—plenty of nursing but no managerial. She wouldn't be able to cope with handling a large staff of receptionists and auxiliary people like counsellors, physios and so on, and a growing patient list.'

'So, who do you favour, Tom?' asked Bill Jones. 'Personally, I'm for Miranda Gibbs, for all the reasons that Kay has given plus some perhaps that she hasn't.' He gave a lazy, lopsided grin. 'You've got to admit that she'd be an ornamental as well as a practical asset to the practice.'

'I second that,' confirmed Val Thorpe, to nobody's surprise. He turned to Brodie, his mobile, handsome, still-boyish face—though he was in his mid-forties—alight and animated. 'You've got to admit, Tom, she's well qualified, as well as being extraordinarily beautiful—and you can't hold that against her.'

'No,' said Tom, 'of course not. And I don't,' he added with more conviction than he felt.

'But I have this gut feeling about her. I still can't see why a career woman of her quality is considering a sideways move, rather than an upward one. The Dorset-born bit almost convinced me but, no, in all fairness I can't go along with the rest of you. I'm giving my vote to Jennifer Harding—a good managerial record, though with a smaller firm, but she's solid and competent and—'

'And very married,' broke in Val, pulling a

face, 'with family ties that might be a drag.'

'Hardly,' said Tom drily. 'Grown-up sons away at university, and a husband working abroad much of the year. Shouldn't be a problem.'

'Agree with that,' said Dennis Withers, raking his fingers through his iron-grey hair. 'Perhaps she would be the safer bet. Understand Tom's reservations about the delectable Miss Gibbs. Move is a bit strange for a dedicated career woman, though she struck me as being entirely above board when she gave her reasons for wanting to join us. I'm going to hold a watching brief for the moment till we consult with the others tonight.'

He stood up. 'Have a surgery in five minutes; see you later.'

He left the room, and soon afterwards so did the other three. They all had surgeries or visits to do, and only Tom was free until the Well Man's clinic at eight.

When they had gone he moved over to the window and, deep in thought, gazed into the busy square below and through the leafy trees towards the cathedral. He noted vaguely that the scaffolding was being dismantled from the honey-gold walls of the ancient building which, over the last few months, had been sandblasted clean. They positively glowed in the afternoon sunshine.

Honey-gold. The colour reminded him of the beautiful Miranda's hair, shining and silky. Impatiently he shook off the thought. Mustn't be distracted by ridiculous fantasies—must try to think rationally.

If the others had their way she would get the job on a majority vote, but he would put up a strong argument in favour of the Jennifer Harding woman, pleasant and a safe bet. Safe for the practice, for she wouldn't arouse any strong feelings.

And, he acknowledged wryly, safe for him personally for she didn't arouse him in the slightest, whereas the delectable Miss Gibbs—as Dennis had called her—stirred up all sorts of feelings he could well do without, feelings he thought he'd squashed long ago.

But if he lost to a majority decision, and Miranda Gibbs was accepted as nurse manager, he would learn to live with it and keep their relationship fairly, but strictly on a professional basis. It might be difficult, but it would be possible. Over the years he'd amicably and successfully avoided any long-term relationship with a number of beautiful women, and there was no reason why he shouldn't do so in this case.

He just wished that the lovely Gibbs woman hadn't intruded and ruffled the status quo of his ordered bachelor existence, which he so valued—though lately there had been times when he'd wondered. . .

With a muttered expletive he cut off his unwelcome train of thought and, turning away from the window, resumed his seat at the table to ponder the problem of Miranda Gibbs.

If only he could find out a little more about her and set his mind at rest as to why she was leaving her present post for a seemingly less prestigious one. Perhaps if he spoke to someone at the Birmingham Health Centre he would get a fuller verbal picture to explain her reasons for moving. He opened the file containing her CV and glowing references.

The five practices serving the health centre headed the top of the page, listing each doctor in each practice. Tom perused them carefully, thinking that there might be a name he recognised from past medical contacts. There was—Laurence McNally. He'd met up with a Laurie McNally on a refresher course a couple of years ago. Could be the same man—he'd take a chance.

He lifted the receiver and phoned the Birmingham number.

'Sorry, Dr Brodie, Dr McNally's not here,' said the

receptionist when he introduced himself and asked to speak to him. 'He's off duty till next week. Can I take a message, or pass you over to one of the other doctors?'

Tom hesitated briefly. Should he speak to someone else? No, his doubts were too nebulous to explain to a complete stranger. He would rather do it in a casual, friendly fashion. 'No, thank you, it doesn't matter. It's nothing urgent—I'll phone again.' He replaced the receiver.

Miranda, determined to put out of her mind the enigmatic Dr Brodie and the possible outcome of her interview, drifted slowly along the cloisters with other tourists toward the entrance to the cathedral proper.

There was an ante-room just outside the door, where pamphlets, pottery and religious *objets d'art* were being sold. She bought a thick, glossy history of the medieval cathedral, using the map it contained to find her way round.

Later she would read it from cover to cover. Right now, all she wanted to do was look and absorb and surrender to the cool, calm beauty of the ancient building, and forget the immediate future.

The nave was glorious. Great carved columns of natural stone decorated with birds, fish and serpents soared upwards, supporting the painted ceiling with great curving arches. Round the walls were stone effigies of long-dead illustrious patrons of the cathedral, saints and martyrs, knights in armour and ladies in wimples—lying side by side on great tombs. The cathedral had a long history.

Dividing the nave from the choir was the central tower, with its south transept and Lady Mary Chapel—the north transept and the Holy Pilgrims Chapel opening from it like two arms of a cross. A framed notice outside the Lady Mary Chapel informed visitors that it was sometimes closed for the conduct of marriage services for local parishioners.

Beyond the choir the elaborately sculpted high altar gleamed with a cloth of gold, silver candlesticks and a mass of flowers. And above the altar rose the brilliant, brash, glass mosaic of a magnificent modern window, all startling blues and golds and clashing pinks—with the legend LET THERE BE LIGHT carved into the stone surround.

Yet somehow it fitted in with the ancient fabric of the cathedral, a contemporary statement of hope and faith.

The scent of flowers and incense hung above the carved pews that filled the floor of the nave and choir. Miranda sat for a while, soaking up the tranquillity of it all—which persisted in spite of the murmuring hum of visitors moving around in little groups.

Leaving by the south-west door some time later, feeling soothed, comforted and elated, she stepped out from the dim doorway into the sunshine.

She was standing on the top step, blinking in the fierce light, when there came a huge, bellowing shout from round the corner of the building, followed by further urgent, loud shouts. And, mingling with the shouts, there came a series of grinding, splintering, metallic noises. Metal clashing on metal. Metal grating against stone, and loud thumps and thuds that made the ground tremble.

A great ball of smoky dust billowed past the front steps.

There was a curious silence for a moment, then more cries and shouts.

A man standing next to Miranda started to run forward. 'Christ,' he exclaimed, 'the scaffolding must've collapsed!'

Her heart rate quickening and adrenalin beginning

to pump, Miranda dashed after the man. Several other people followed her.

They rounded the corner in a little bunch, and momentarily came to a halt as they surveyed the scene before them. Poles and chains, planks of splintered wood and small chunks of masonry lay strewn all over the ground, where the scaffolding had been torn from the side of the building.

But a few planks and poles were still hanging crazily to the cathedral wall at an acute angle. A man was clinging to the tilting platform some thirty feet up.

There were bodies lying on the ground, half-concealed by planks, iron poles and torn plastic sheeting. Frighteningly inert mounds. Two yellow-hatted men were tearing chunks of stone and metal from one of the mounds. A third man was calling up to the man on the scaffolding and manoeuvring a ladder along the wall toward him.

A veil of dust hung over everything.

'Give a hand,' shouted one of the workmen as Miranda and the others appeared. 'There's a couple of other blokes over there.' He indicated two other piles of debris.

Miranda made for the nearest heap of metal and wood and broken masonry. A man's sturdy brown legs and firm buttocks, clad in brief shorts, protruded from the rubble that partly concealed his torso and head. Carefully Miranda removed the jagged stones and pieces of piping. He was lying prone, his head—what she could see of it—to one side, his exposed cheek bleeding from a deep cut.

A heavy plank was lying across his bare shoulders and the back of his head. She began to heave at the plank and somebody joined her, lifting the other end until, together, they managed to manoeuvre it off the injured man.

His hard hat had been knocked sideways. Blood was leaking steadily from a large pulpy wound on the back and top of his head. Miranda knelt down and automatically felt for the pulse by his exposed ear, from which a trickle of clear fluid oozed. It was faint, uneven and rapid. He was unconscious, but breathing. She knew at once that there was not a lot she could do, except cover the wound to prevent more dust and dirt getting in.

She reached for her bag lying nearby where she had dropped it and fished out a clean tissue, which she laid gently over the pulpy mess. Then she swiftly folded another tissue into a pad and placed it over the exposed ear, noting as she did so that the clear fluid was now slightly blood-streaked.

The man who had helped her move the plank said shakily, 'God, what a bloody mess. Shouldn't we turn him over so that he can breathe better? His face is half-buried.' His own face was rather pale.

'No, we mustn't move him,' she said sharply. 'I think he's got a fractured skull and perhaps a spinal injury; he's lying at an awkward angle. We must wait for the ambulance people.'

'You sure—you a doctor or something?' He sounded suspicious, rather belligerent.

'I'm an experienced nurse,' said Miranda firmly. 'Trust me, I know what I am talking about. Look, you go and help some of the others. I'll stay here and make sure that nobody tries to move him.'

'OK, if you're sure. . .'

'Positive.'

He looked relieved as he moved off.

Head wounds, reflected Miranda as he walked away, were always messy and particularly unpleasant. No wonder the poor man looked shaken.

She was aware of small shards of stone piercing her knees, and eased them up one at a time. She seemed to have been kneeling for a long time, though it could only have been minutes, when Dr Brodie appeared quietly at the other side of the inert body.

Miranda was inordinately pleased to see him.

'Saw what happened from the surgery window,' he explained briefly. 'Ambulance has been alerted. What's going on here?' He crouched down on his haunches.

'Head wound. Fractured skull, I think—typical discharge from ear and nose. Pulse feeble and rapid. And I'm not sure about his neck or spine. Could be damaged. Thought I'd better stay to make sure that he doesn't move or that nobody tries to move him, but there's not much else I can do.'

He nodded, carefully lifted a corner of the tissue and looked at the bloody mass of bone and tissue beneath. He pulled a face.

'Not much *anyone* can do,' he muttered. 'Let's hope he makes it to Casualty.' He shone a pencil torch beam into the unconscious man's one exposed eye. 'Pinpoint pupil; other one's probably dilated. You're right about a fracture—keep him immobile. His breathing's not too bad, considering; make sure his airways stay clear. Give me a shout if he comes round. I'm going to see if there's anything I can do for any of these other chaps.'

He smiled suddenly, a wide, warm smile, and said softly, 'Good job you were around to stop him being moved. Could have been fatal.'

He unfolded himself and stood up—very tall, very lean—straightened wide, well-muscled shoulders that strained against his silk shirt then, with a nod, turned and moved away with long easy strides, picking his way with sure steps across the rubble.

Miranda stared at his receding back, sorry to see him go. His brief appearance and confirmation of her own assessment of the injured man had been reassuring.

Moments later somebody else took up his place,

crouching down as he had done. Young, ribbon-skinny in tight jeans, he had a spotty face, a shock of red hair and was holding a camera.

'Reporter photographer, *Minster Echo*,' he introduced himself, sounding brash and indecently cheerful. 'I'm here to take pics. Can I look underneath here?' He stretched out a hand to lift the tissue.

'No, you damn well can't,' Miranda spat out, and smacked his hand away. 'That's to keep the dirt off.'

He shrugged. 'I only asked,' he said. 'He looks in a pretty bad way. Is he unconscious?'

'Yes.'

'Why don't you turn him over and make him more comfortable? He's practically eating dirt.'

'Because he mustn't be moved as long as he can breathe, except by the paramedics who are trained for this and have the right equipment.'

The youth shrugged. 'Emergency stuff, like in *Casualty*. You a nurse?'

'Yes.'

'Mind telling me your name?'

'Yes, I do mind. Look, why don't you take your picture if you must, and then go away? There's a man hanging onto the scaffolding. Why don't you take a picture of him—much more interesting?'

'Done that. Got some smashing pics. But he's not gonna fall. They're putting up ladders to get him down. I was passing when all this happened. First on the scene, saw it all, great, real scoop.' He grinned. 'My editor's going to love this.' He stood up, aimed the camera at Miranda and the unconscious man and clicked it several times.

Miranda snorted. 'Ghoul,' she snarled. 'Why don't you go and do something useful, like help with the rescue?'

'OK, keep cool; only doing my job, lady,' he

said sulkily, and turned and walked away.

Miranda turned her attention back to the injured man, wiped the trickle of fluid from his nose and took his pulse again. Still the same—weak, thready, fast—and, in spite of the heat, his skin was cold and clammy. Pulling off her thin linen jacket, she tucked it over his grazed, sweaty back. It was the best she could do.

She glanced hopefully at the little circle of spectators who had come out of the cathedral and were being held back by a solitary policeman—everyone was in summer dresses and shirtsleeves.

It was at that moment that she heard the sound of sirens close by. Thank God—ambulances and more police.

There were two ambulances. One crunched to a halt on the gravel nearby, and two paramedics climbed out and crouched down beside her. 'OK love, we'll take over,' one of them said, gently shoving her aside. He carefully lifted the tissues covering the wound and the ear. 'You've done the right thing, covering this up. Guess you're in the business.'

Miranda nodded. 'Nurse,' she explained.

Echoing the doctor's words, the other paramedic said, 'Good job you were around to stop anyone moving him. Could have caused problems, to say the least.'

He introduced an airway into the injured man's mouth and held an oxygen mask over his mouth and nose, while his colleague replaced the paper tissues covering the suppurating ear and head wound with protective pads. Then, as one set up a fluid line into the patient's hand, the other skillfully placed a padded collar round his neck and replaced Miranda's jacket with a foil sheet.

She held the flask feeding the line as the ambulance team, with infinite care, eased the man onto a stretcher.

Everything was done with smooth, swift efficiency.

It was all over in an incredibly short while and, siren wailing, the ambulance moved off down the cathedral drive into the square.

CHAPTER TWO

ONCE the ambulance had gone Miranda realised that there was nothing else she could do.

She looked across the rubble-strewn ground to where the other two injured workmen were being attended to by the paramedics manning the second ambulance. There was quite a lot of activity going on there. She could see Dr Brodie working with the paramedics, crouching over first one and then the other casualty.

The workman who had been clinging to the scaffolding had been brought down to the ground, and was standing at the foot of a ladder being photographed by the reporter from the *Echo*. The other policemen who had arrived were dispersing the crowd that had gathered.

A senior officer, distinguished by the silver pips on his shoulders, was talking to the men in hard hats who were pointing up at the wall and the remaining scaffolding, evidently explaining what had happened.

Redundant, thought Miranda wryly. No one needs me; might as well go. Everyone was busy, except her. She felt a little prickle of regret that she wasn't able to say goodbye to the doctor. He'd been so reassuring and friendly when she'd been attending the injured man.

She folded her creased and grubby strawberry-pink jacket over her arm, picked up her shoulder-bag and made to leave. A police sergeant came over and spoke to her.

'Are you all right, miss?' he asked. 'I understand you took care of one of the injured men with a nasty head wound. That couldn't have been very pleasant.'

'No, it wasn't, but I'm a nurse and I've seen worse. I just hope the poor chap gets safely to hospital. He stands a chance with intensive care.'

'Poor devil, have to keep our fingers crossed for him. I'm sure his chances would have been less if you'd not been around. Trouble is, we can't afford to get too involved in our jobs whatever we feel, can we?'

Miranda shook her head. 'Try not to,' she said, 'but it isn't always easy.'

'Nope. By the way, Nurse, how are you going to get home?'

'Walk. I'm staying at The Mitre—it's not far.'

'The other side of town. If you don't mind my saying so, you look a bit of a mess. You can't walk about like that. I'm sure we can give you a lift.'

'Oh.' Miranda looked down at her dirty, crumpled skirt and torn stockings. She pulled a face, and said ruefully, 'I hadn't realised. You're right, I do look a fright.'

The sergeant grinned, his eyes glinting with frank admiration. 'I didn't say that. I'd say that it was impossible for you to look a fright,' he said, mildly flirtatious. 'But you definitely need a tidy-up. Stay there; I'll fix up a car to take you to the hotel.'

'No need, Sergeant,' said Dr Brodie, suddenly materialising beside him. 'I've finished here. I'll take Miss Gibbs back.'

'Oh, so you know this lady, Doc?' The sergeant grinned at Miranda and shrugged theatrically. 'Pity. My loss is the doctor's gain. It would have been my pleasure to have given you a lift.'

'And mine to accept it,' smiled Miranda, playing up to him. 'Thank you.'

The sergeant offered her a sketchy salute. 'I'll be off, then, and leave you in Doc Brodie's hands.' He winked. 'You can trust him—he's our locum police surgeon and has to behave himself,' he quipped with heavy humour, and with a nod to them both moved off to join a group of officers nearby.

Miranda turned to the doctor. 'Are you sure you've got the time to take me back to the hotel? Haven't you a surgery or visits to make?'

The doctor's dark brown eyes bored into hers. He raised an expressive eyebrow. 'Managing me already, Miss Gibbs?' he asked laconically, his mouth twitching at the corners.

Miranda—who didn't often blush—found herself flushing, for no good reason that she could think of. 'Wouldn't dream of it,' she said sharply. 'I just know how busy you must be. It's kind of you to offer.'

Dr Brodie shrugged. 'Not at all; least I can do,' he said briskly. 'After all, had you not been at the interview. . .' his voice trailed off and he waved an expressive hand at the debris lying around them, 'you wouldn't have been involved in this little lot and ruined a perfectly good pair of tights, or stockings, or whatever. I feel rather responsible.'

'Well, you don't have to,' said Miranda. 'You should have let that nice police sergeant take me back to the hotel. He was only too willing.'

The doctor put a hand under her elbow and began to propel her down the drive, away from the cathedral. 'And I'm only too willing,' he said firmly. 'End of discussion. And, before you accuse me of neglecting my duty, let me tell you that I have nothing on except paperwork till the Well Man's clinic at eight.'

'Oh, well, in that case. . .thank you, Dr Brodie.' She gave him a brilliant smile as they threaded their way across the busy square.

Tom stared down at her and almost came to a halt, dazzled by the sheer beauty of her smile which lit up her face and was reflected in her laughing green eyes. Get a grip on yourself, man, he told himself. So she's beautiful. So what? You don't have to let her bewitch you. Pull yourself together!

He pulled himself together, tightened his grasp on her arm and steered her to where his car was parked in the centre car park.

Miranda was pondering on what she had said or done to make him frown so fiercely when they stopped beside a gleaming, newly registered black Range Rover.

'Oh, lovely—super car,' she said enthusiastically. Surely that would wipe the frown from his face. Men loved to have their cars admired. 'Chunky but sleek, dependable—a go-anywhere vehicle, I always think. You can keep your Porsches and your Jags, and give me a Range Rover any day.' She laughed and added, almost shyly, 'I've got a thing about them—Range Rovers. My father drove one when I was a small girl. There weren't so many about then and I used to feel very grand, lording it above the other cars. I could see everything.'

She spoke with an easy naturalness and simplicity that surprised Brodie. This was not the coolly elegant, sophisticated woman whom he had so short a time ago interviewed and who had more than vaguely disquieted him. Nor the practical, caring nurse who had knelt, unmindful of her stockings or skirt, in the dust and tended the injured workman. This was a combination of the two women, with an added dimension of warmth and humour and a kind of innocence thrown in, enhancing her purely physical beauty.

Perhaps he had been wrong about her—made a hasty judgement when he had cast her in the role of a sort of *femme fatale*, whose very beauty would disrupt their day-to-day lives. Mentally he shrugged. Oh, well, if she did get the vote and joined the practice somehow he would have to steel himself to guard against her particular brand of sex appeal.

But, by God, it was going to be difficult. Those almond-shaped, laughing eyes, those tendrils of honey-gold hair against the lightly tanned, swan-like neck. . .

Savagely he squashed his sensual thoughts and made himself concentrate on her practical qualities. At least, now that he had seen her at work in the field he had no fears about her hands-on nursing ability—she certainly had the right attitude to that.

He gave her a glimmer of a smile as he opened the door of the car, and Miranda smiled widely back. Thank goodness he'd stopped glowering, she thought as she climbed into the passenger seat.

'There are cleansing wipes in the glove compartment. Do help yourself,' he offered as he closed the door on her, walked round to the driver's side and slid into his seat.

'Thanks.' She found them, and scrubbed at her grubby hands.

He fastened his seat belt, put the car into gear and edged out into the busy street. 'Well, you're obviously a Range Rover enthusiast, but I take it that you don't drive one yourself,' he guessed.

Miranda pulled a face. 'I should be so lucky. Way beyond my pocket, both to buy and maintain. No, no Range Rover for me. I'm the proud owner of an elderly, but much-loved Mini that I've had since it was a baby and goes like a bomb.'

'One careful lady owner,' said the doctor, not sarcastically—as she momentarily suspected—but with a nice, lopsided smile. He added approvingly, 'Nice little cars, Minis, but I find them a bit on the small size. I like the space a Rover gives me, and it's ideal for visiting our out-of-town surgeries and some of our country patients. The hilly terrain round here can be dicey in the winter.'

They drove in silence for a few minutes, smoothly following the intricate one-way system that wove through the centre of town toward the outskirts and The Mitre Hotel. Miranda studied her companion's lean, tanned hands as they rested in a relaxed fashion on the wheel. Nice hands, she thought, firm and sure—good doctor's hands.

It reminded her of how carefully he had lifted the covering from the injured workman's head, and she asked abruptly, 'How do you think they'll do—those men who were hurt?'

He flicked a glance sideways at her, and then quickly turned his attention back to the road.

'They should be OK,' he said thoughtfully. 'At least the two I was helping with should. One of them has a fractured femur and humerus; the other was briefly concussed and has some rib damage and lots of cuts and bruises, and there's an outside chance of internal injuries but nothing definite. Your chap's a different matter. Don't hold out much hope for him—he looked in a pretty bad way, didn't he?'

'Afraid so, poor man. I wonder if he is married with children.' Her voice was soft.

'Does it make it worse if he's got kids? After all, a life's a life. Surely as a professional you accept that, and it's our job to save lives.' He sounded sharp and coolly impersonal.

His coolness surprised her. Was he one of those doctors who distanced themselves from their patients, never allowed themselves to get close? Correct, but coldly clinical? How disappointing!

'Of course,' she replied stiffly. 'Any life is important, but if there are children deprived of a father or mother, for whatever reason, it somehow seems more tragic—

leaving a parent to cope on his or her own. Well, I suppose I'm old-fashioned, but I think children need both parents around when they're growing up.'

'In an ideal world,' said the doctor so harshly that Miranda turned to look at him, and saw that his face looked suddenly grim and remote. She looked away hastily, somehow feeling as if she was intruding on private, unhappy thoughts.

Moments later, smoothly negotiating the last busy roundabout, he turned into the wide, gravelled forecourt of The Mitre Hotel—a large, unusually attractive Victorian building, covered in Virginia creeper.

They stopped at the foot of the steps leading up to the impressive heavy swing-doors, all decorated plate-glass panels and dark wood. The doctor unfastened his seat belt as Miranda fumbled with hers, and had his hand on the doorhandle when she said quietly, 'Please don't get out, Doctor. Thanks for bringing me back. You've been very kind.'

She might as well have saved her breath, for before she had freed herself of the seat belt and gathered up her jacket and bag which had slid to the floor he was round her side of the car and opening the passenger door.

'I'll see you in,' he said in a no-nonsense voice and, taking her arm, steered her up the steps. 'Room number?' he asked when they reached the old-fashioned reception lounge, with its potted palms, easy chairs and low tables.

'Thirty, but, really, there's no need.'

He took no notice but collected her key, propelled her into the lift—which was fortunately empty—and pressed the first-floor button.

Although she had protested, conscious of her torn stockings and grubby skirt and a film of whitish dust over her hair and face, Miranda was grateful for the doctor's presence as they walked down the wide, thickly carpeted corridor. He was dusty too, she noted, though not as badly as she, presumably because she had been kneeling down as the worst of the dust settled immediately following the collapse of the scaffolding.

They met one or two people leaving their rooms, who looked with some surprise at Miranda before quickly averting their eyes, and she was especially glad to feel the increased pressure of Dr Brodie's hand on her arm.

He unlocked the door when they reached her room, opened it wide and pushed her firmly through. 'Go and have a stiff drink, wash your hair and have a nice long hot soak,' he ordered. 'You deserve it, and you certainly need it.' He touched her cheek lightly, his fingertips brushing at the dust. 'And don't dwell on what happened. It's over and done with. You did your bit. You were splendid.'

Then suddenly brisk, he added, almost impatiently, 'Goodnight, Miss Gibbs. You'll hear from us in the morning,' and, with a nod, turned abruptly and strode away down the corridor toward the lift.

A little taken aback by his sudden curtness and feeling vaguely lost after he had departed, Miranda closed the door and stood leaning thoughtfully against it for a moment. What a strange man, full of contradictions—kind and considerate one moment, taciturn and dismissive the next. And yet she liked him; was reassured by him; was sorry to see him go. How odd to have such feelings about someone she had just met and who didn't seem to like her much.

She crossed the room to the window to catch a final glimpse of him as he left the building. And it *would* be final, she thought sadly, if she didn't get the job.

She stared down into the forecourt as the doctor emerged through the swing-doors and ran down the steps. Her heart beat a little tattoo against her chest at the sight of him and her breathing quickened. She put a hand to her throat—what on earth was happening to her?

He must have had his keys at the ready, for he opened the door of the Range Rover immediately. But he paused as he was about to climb aboard, and glanced up and along the first-floor windows until he located Miranda's room.

Hastily she made to step back into the shadows, but he had seen her and raised his hand in a casual farewell salute. She had no option but to wave back and then stand and watch as he drove away.

'Damn,' she said aloud. Her cheeks flushed with annoyance. What on earth must he have thought, seeing her standing at the window obviously waiting for him to leave? Is that why he had looked up—because he had been conscious of her watching him? Why else had he searched for her window?

'How pathetic and humiliating. I'm behaving like a besotted schoolgirl,' she muttered and, crossing to the drinks cabinet, poured herself a medicinal brandy as the doctor had ordered.

Tom Brodie was plagued by similar uncomfortable thoughts as he drove away from the hotel.

What the devil had the lovely Miranda thought when she'd seen him staring up at her window? Had she realised that he had been searching for her room, or had she assumed that he was simply admiring the graceful façade of the old building?

He swore savagely under his breath. What a hope. He *must* have given himself away. She must have seen through him and, well aware of the effect she had on men, at this moment be despising him for behaving like an infatuated fool. Bloody hell, how had he let himself sink to such depths as to moon around after a beautiful woman whom he'd only just met?

It was ludicrous!

No, it wasn't ludicrous; that was the point. There was nothing in the least bit funny about the situation. He was more than attracted to Miranda Gibbs—he was in danger of falling in love with her.

In love with her!

Nonsense. Impossible! But it wasn't impossible. She'd drawn him like a magnet from the moment she'd entered the room for her interview. Bowled him over, staggered him with her beauty, made his palms sweat. He, the sophisticated, experienced bachelor. And it had got worse as the interview progressed and he had fired almost impossible questions at her, deliberately trying to trip her up—seeking to find a flaw in her cool composure.

He hadn't succeeded, even though as a final resort he had queried her reasons for wanting to join the practice. Every lift of her chin, turn of her head and glance from her amazing green eyes had underlined her serenity, her professionalism. She was as intelligent as she was beautiful and, as Kay Brent had pointed out, possessed of a delightful sense of humour.

She was a rounded woman, a complete woman. No other woman of his acquaintance had made such an impact on him—ever. He groaned. If she came into the practice and he was to survive without making a fool of himself he was going to have to play it cool, very cool, somehow without damaging their working relationship.

It wasn't until he was almost back at the surgery that it occurred to him to wonder what she had been doing at the window! His hands, usually relaxed when he was driving, tightened on the wheel, his heart beat a little faster and his pulse rate quickened. Could she have been there because she had wanted to see him leave? Was it possible? Could she be attracted to him. . .?

His heart and pulse did more peculiar things as he considered the possibility, and he was late signalling that he was turning into the surgery car park. The driver of the car behind him hooted stridently and he gestured an apology, before swerving into the paved area and parking in the space reserved for staff.

He sat for a few minutes, staring unseeingly down at his hands still on resting on the steering-wheel, as he fought to come to terms with the extraordinary situation in which he found himself.

Here he was, attracted to a woman whose motives for wanting to move to Combe Minster were vaguely suspect. And if those suspicions were justified, and he learned something to that effect from Lawrence McNally in Birmingham, what the hell should he do about it—keep it to himself or share it with his colleagues?

And, when it came down to it, what was he suspicious about? There was nothing tangible. Her references made it clear that she was squeaky-clean professionally, and he didn't doubt this for an instant. His suspicions circled round her beauty and the peculiar feeling he had that it had something to do with her wanting to leave Birmingham, and the fear that it might in some way affect the practice.

The cathedral clock chimed seven-thirty, rousing him out of his reverie. Time to wash and brush up and change his shirt before his clinic.

He retrieved his medical bag from the back seat and, ruthlessly squashing his disturbing thoughts, made his way to his consulting-room to prepare for the evening ahead of him. An evening that would end with the medical staff meeting and the vote to appoint the new nurse manager. Well, whatever he learned, if anything, from McNally would be too late to influence the voting.

Strengthened and calmed by the brandy, Miranda thought long and hard about Dr Brodie and her reaction to him as she showered and shampooed her hair then lay in a scented bath and soaked. Why had he made such a strong impression on her, far more than any of the other doctors on the interview panel? They had all been quite forceful characters and had had plenty to say, pertinent questions to ask and yet had been quite friendly.

In varying degrees they had all presented attractive personalities, so why on earth did she feel drawn to him when he had made it plain that he didn't approve of her—not as a candidate for the post of nurse manager, or as a woman? He seemed downright suspicious of her and, unlike the other men, apparently unmoved by her beauty.

There had been a moment during the interview when he'd been faintly bothered by it, but the moment of hesitation had passed and he had continued with his belligerent questioning. Well, great, she wanted this job on merit, nothing else.

True, he had been a little less frosty by the end of the interview, but she had taken that as a sop to good manners rather than a reversal of his opinion of her. He was still, as far as she could tell, against her as a responsible employee of the practice.

He had been considerate and courteous to her since her involvement in the accident, but had made it plain that this was because he felt a responsibility toward her because of her vague connection with the practice.

There was no doubt about it—for some reason his feelings for her were not friendly and she certainly couldn't depend on his vote. But, with luck, she could depend on the other doctors who had interviewed her to vote in her favour and convince their absent colleagues that she was the right person for the job.

And if she got the job that she so coveted in the face of Thomas Brodie's opposition, how would they get along with each other on a day-to-day basis? Silly question—they were both professionals and would behave with complete professionalism. She was drawn to him, liked him but would keep that liking under wraps and play it cool. He didn't like her but she was sure that he wouldn't let that fact interfere with work.

There was one good thing about his antipathy, she reflected as she got out of the cooling bath, there wouldn't be a repeat of the situation she was leaving behind in Birmingham. She wasn't going to have the effect on Dr Brodie that she'd unwittingly had on poor Steven. *He* was clearly immune to her charms, thank God.

As for the other men in the practice, she would keep them at arm's length—be friendly, nothing more.

She made a face at herself in the mirror, and murmured ruefully to her reflection, 'That is, if you get the job. It isn't the bag yet.'

In spite of being tired after the trauma and excitement of the day, Miranda didn't sleep very well. She lay awake worrying about the victims of the accident, especially the man for whom she had made herself responsible. Had he survived the night? If he survived, would he be brain-damaged? Was he married with children who would be deprived of a father if he died? And why had Dr Brodie reacted so oddly when she had put forward that possibility?

She mulled over the thought, seeing in her mind's eye the doctor's face when she had suggested this. It had borne a closed, bleak expression.

Had he suffered a loss, perhaps been left a widower

with motherless children? Or was he divorced and separated from his wife and family and desperately unhappy about it? What nonsense! She was letting her imagination run away with her. Probably he was happily married and she had imagined his anguished look when she had spoken of the trauma of children being deprived of a parent.

Married! The idea brought her up with a jolt. But why should it surprise her that Dr Brodie might be married? It was the most likely scenario for a man of his age. Not that it mattered one way or the other, for heaven's sake; his personal life was his own. She was only interested in him as a doctor and perhaps her future boss, not as a man.

That wasn't quite true, she had to admit. Against her will, she had felt instantly drawn to him and knew that she would rather have him for her friend than her enemy. . . No, enemy was too strong a word. She just wished that he didn't dislike her as much as he appeared to do.

But perhaps she was wrong about that. Maybe he was normally taciturn with strangers. After all, she knew so little about him. She knew that he was a senior GP in the practice, since his name was listed immediately beneath that of the elderly Dr Withers who was the head of practice and would soon be retiring. Presumably Dr Brodie would then take over as head of practice, which was why he had taken charge of the interview.

Her compulsive thoughts wouldn't let her mind rest. She went over and over the details of her interview. Could she have given more intelligent answers to the questions that had been fired at her by the five doctors?

The euphoria that she had experienced in the cathedral, when she had felt sure that she would get the job, had disappeared and she was plagued with doubts. Sadly, she must accept that if the imperious Dr Brodie had his way she certainly wouldn't be appointed nurse manager in the cathedral practice.

For, whatever friendly feelings she had for him, he'd made it clear that he had none for her. He was, at best, neutral. Even when, with distant courtesy, he had escorted her back to the hotel he had made it plain that only duty had compelled him to do so.

And it was on this last depressing thought that she drifted into an uneasy sleep.

Brilliant August sunshine was streaming into her room through the heavy cotton curtains when Miranda woke. Her busy mind went into action the moment she opened her eyes. Her stomach fluttered in anticipation of what the day might bring, her mind darting from one possibility to the other—would she get the job; wouldn't she get the job?

It was ridiculous and out of character to be so worked up, she told herself. If she didn't get this particular post she would apply for one of the others for which she had been short-listed.

But she didn't want any other job; she wanted this one, with all the challenges that it had to offer—a newly created post that she could make all her own. She had fallen in love with this bustling little city with its ancient, elegant cathedral and historic buildings, and wanted to live and work in Combe Minster.

She took a needle-cold shower to shock herself into a more rational state of mind. Then aware that if she *was* accepted for the job—she crossed her fingers—she would be called for another interview, she put on her make-up with great care and turned her attention to what she should wear.

From the limited wardrobe that she had brought with her, mostly containing holiday clothes, she chose a calf-length dark tan skirt, matching jacket with broad cream lapels and tan medium-heeled sandals. She eyed herself in the mirror and was satisfied—fine, casually businesslike, but needing a touch of colour. She fastened a striking brooch of green and gold enamel to one lapel and hooked tiny matching enamelled earrings into her small, neat lobes.

The final touch—perfect.

'You'll do, Miranda Gibbs,' she told her mirror image. 'Just stay cool and don't let the formidable Dr Brodie rattle you. He is, after all, only a man.' And, with this bit of morale-boosting, she gathered up her bag and room key and made her way down to the dining-room for breakfast.

Determined not to rush back to her room and sit waiting for the phone to ring, she dawdled over grapefruit and kedgeree, toast and marmalade and a large pot of surprisingly good aromatic coffee. She browsed through a morning newspaper without really taking in what she was reading, then checked her watch—nine o'clock. Any time now there might be a call from the surgery. Dr Brodie had promised that she would be informed by eleven, 'one way or another,' he had said.

She returned to her room.

The phone was ringing as she opened the door. So soon! Breathing rapidly, her heart pounding and her hand trembling slightly, she picked up the receiver.

'Hello.'

'Miss Gibbs?' enquired a woman's detached voice, totally devoid of expression.

'Speaking.' She was proud of the steadiness in her own voice. Was this the brush-off, or. . .

'This is Dr Brodie's receptionist speaking. Hold on, please, I have Dr Brodie on the line for you.'

'Thank you.' Well, at least he was going to give her the news himself but, then, he wasn't the sort of man to shy away from his responsibilities.

'Morning, Miss Gibbs.' He sounded brisk and efficient.

'Good morning, Dr Brodie.' Thank God, not a tremble.

'I trust you slept well after yesterday's traumas.'

Stuffy, very formal. He was being polite, not a good sign. He was going to break it to her gently that she hadn't got the job.

'Fine,' she lied. 'I took your advice, had a stiff drink, a hot bath and slept like the proverbial log.'

'Good. And thank you once again for helping out with the casualties. By the way, your man survived the night. I rang the hospital—I thought you'd like to know. They've operated and he's in with a chance.'

'That's marvellous; thank you for telling me.'

'Not at all.' There was a minuscule pause and then he said brusquely, 'But the real reason that I'm ringing, Miss Gibbs, is to let you know the result of your interview and confirm your appointment as nurse manager to the practice. Congratulations and, on behalf of myself and my colleagues, welcome to Combe Minster.'

Her heart missed several beats. She'd got it; got the job.

She exhaled soundlessly. And he'd welcomed her, a stiff welcome but a welcome of sorts. But she'd got the job and that was all that mattered. She suppressed a desire to let out a shriek of joy and said evenly, 'Well, thank you, thank you very much, Dr Brodie. I'm delighted, very pleased. I look forward to joining the practice.'

'And we look forward to having you; there's a lot of work to be done on the management front—you'll have plenty to do to get things organised. I'd like to tie up your contract as soon as possible. Can you come over this morning to discuss details and so on, and at the same time I can show you around and introduce you to a few people?'

'I can drive over immediately.'

'In your much-cherished Mini?' he asked, a hint of laughter in his voice.

'In my beloved Mini.'

'Park in the staff bay at the side of the house.'

'Will do. Goodbye. Be with you shortly, Dr Brodie.'

'Fine. See you soon, Miss Gibbs; ask for me in Reception and they'll give me a buzz.'

Half an hour later she arrived at the practice premises, Regency House. It was a spacious, cream, flat-fronted town house, aptly named for the period, surrounded by a large garden which was mostly paved or gravelled with a border of trees and shrubs and a cobbled wall.

She parked where instructed by the doctor, walked round to the front entrance and let herself into Reception.

Yesterday, keyed up for her interview, she had hardly noticed her surroundings but now she looked round with interest.

A capacious ground-floor room of the elegant building had been converted to form a rather grand waiting-room and reception area. Behind a large horseshoe-shaped counter, laden with a computer terminal and several telephones, were racks of pigeon-holes containing patient's notes. A short, plump woman was balanced on a small stepladder, reaching up for a file.

Miranda raised her eyebrows. Something would have to be done about those files—they would be a priority.

She crossed to the desk and stood behind a couple of people, waiting for attention. The two patients before her were dealt with, and the neatly coiffured receptionist turned to her and smiled. 'Can I help?' she enquired politely.

'I have an appointment to see Dr Brodie—'

The receptionist interrupted, 'I'm sorry, Dr Brodie's not on duty this morning.'

'I'm not a patient. My name's Gibbs, Miranda Gibbs.'

The professional smile on the receptionist's face became fixed, her voice chilly.

'Oh, Miss Gibbs. Yes, the doctor is expecting you.' She glanced at the small telephone switchboard. 'He's on an outside line at the moment. I'll let him know that you're here as soon as he's free. Will you please take a seat?'

The brush-off, thought Miranda; she knows or guesses who I am and resents a newcomer. Oh, well, all par for the course. I'll have to work hard to win her over. 'Thank you,' she said pleasantly.

She found a seat as directed on one of the chrome and leather chairs lining the walls, and immediately found herself in conversation with her next-door neighbour about the trials and tribulations of leg ulcers.

On the floor above, in his consulting-room, Tom Brodie had just finished his phone call to Lawrence McNally in Birmingham and was sitting staring into space, mulling over the conversation.

It had not been a very satisfactory conversation—he had learned very little about Miranda that he didn't already know.

Yes, her extraordinary beauty had initially caused some hassle, agreed McNally to an obliquely-put question, but that had soon resolved itself and she had won over most of the staff. She was a super manager and the group co-operative hadn't wanted to lose her and had offered her an increased salary to stay, but she had been adamant about going.

For personal or professional reasons? Tom had probed gently. A little of both, thought McNally guardedly. Miranda and one of his colleagues had had something going between them, but it had come to nothing. Why, he had no idea. Neither had been forthcoming about the affair. That was all Larry McNally could or was prepared to tell him, apart from repeating that he could thoroughly recommend Miranda for the post that was on offer in Combe Minster.

Tom thought over what he had been told. It was clear that the lovely Miranda had had another reason for leaving the Birmingham job, other than the one she had given, as he had suspected. But had she left because she was broken-hearted, or had she left a broken heart—perhaps more than one—behind her? And was it significant and did it matter as long as she didn't cause havoc here in Combe Minster?

His colleagues had voted her into the practice, and he had no option but to accept that. It would be up to him to make sure that neither they nor she suspected that his feelings were already involved to an absurd degree that astonished and angered him. How the hell had he let this happen—at his age and with his experience of women?

Well, it *had* happened, he thought grimly, but as long as she never guessed he could deal with it, and to this end he would adopt a coolly professional attitude toward her at all times.

His internal phone rang. He lifted the receiver. 'Yes?'

'Miss Gibbs is here, Dr Brodie,' announced the receptionist.

Tom inhaled deeply. 'Right, please send her up, Mrs Payne,' he said in an expressionless voice.

'Will do, Doctor.' She put down the receiver and called out imperiously, 'Miss Gibbs, Dr Brodie will see you now,' and, as Miranda stood up, added sharply, 'His room's first floor, second door on the left.'

Refusing to be fazed by her abruptness, Miranda gave her a brilliant smile. 'Thank you,' she said and, without haste, turned and made her way up the wide staircase for her meeting with the doctor.

CHAPTER THREE

MIRANDA moved into number five Almond Terrace, Combe Minster, four hectic weeks later.

They were frantically busy weeks spent packing, working out the remainder of her notice left over from her holiday, breaking in her assistant as manager of the centre and arranging to relet her flat.

By the eve of her departure she was exhausted and feeling rather deflated. To her surprise, she found that although she was glad to be leaving Birmingham and was looking forward immensely to her new job she was a little sad too. Initially she had enjoyed her work at the large health centre with its daily challenges.

But Steven had spoiled that. If only he hadn't recently become so obsessed and turned their easygoing friendship into something deadly serious—something that required a commitment that she wasn't ready to give—she might have renewed her contract.

Not that for an instant did she now regret her decision to move. Her moment of sadness passed. A flutter of joy flickered through her. She couldn't wait to get down to Dorset—returning to her roots, as Dr Brodie had suggested.

The enigmatic Dr Brodie! Try as she might, she couldn't stop him from popping in and out of her thoughts. He had been freezingly polite at their last meeting when they had tied up her contract and sorted out the details of her duties.

His image as he had sat at his desk, talking to her in his deep but—on that occasion—steely voice, niggled at her: the lean clever face beneath the thick black hair; the dark brown eyes surveying her thoughtfully from behind horn-rimmed spectacles; the raised eyebrows and the wide, sardonic mouth that occasionally quirked into the glimmer of a smile.

The smooth way he had distanced himself from her that morning after his thoughtfulness the previous evening had disappointed but not surprised her. She had half expected him to adopt just such an attitude and, indeed, in a peculiar way, welcomed it. For being cool and professional was how she intended to be herself in her future dealings with him.

But *his* coolness had been tempered by the warm welcome given her by his medical colleagues and most of the other staff to whom she had been introduced.

There had been exceptions. Pat Payne, the senior receptionist who had spoken to her on her arrival at the surgery, had scarcely tried to veil her hostility. And Liz Fuller, the senior nursing sister, had been even more hostile. It was a pity, but understandable. As the two most senior members of staff they probably resented someone being brought in over their heads; perhaps felt that they could continue to run the newly extended practice without a manager.

But their hostility had only served to whet Miranda's appetite to exploit her management skills, and she couldn't wait to take up her post. Given time, she felt confident that she would win them over, both of them, and any other staff who might initially resent her.

For she got on well with people, men and women, once they got to know her and understood that she didn't flaunt her beauty or misuse it. She would weld them all together—doctors, nurses, receptionists and visiting ancillary staff—into a perfect, efficient, happy team, geared to the care of their patients. The cathedral practice would become renowned as a medical centre of excellence.

On the day she moved into number five the reddening leaves of the almond trees that lined the terrace were fluttering down before a gusting wind. And it was pouring with rain, but neither wind nor rain could spoil the old-world charm of the tile-hung cottages and their pretty front gardens behind low cobbled walls.

The almond blossoms would be fabulous in the spring, she thought, staring out through the rain-spattered, diamond-leaded panes of the sitting-room across her own tiny garden rioting with colour. There were late crimson roses and purple Michaelmas daisies, amber chrysanthemums and brilliant pink asters. Even through the rain they glowed.

She had been lucky to lease number five. According to the house agent, properties in the terrace didn't often come on the market to rent and tenants were strictly vetted. She had passed the acid test by providing excellent solicitor's, banker's and previous employer's references. Part-furnished, leaving room for her own precious pieces, it was a delightful gem of a cottage—one of ten tucked away in a little mews in the shadow of the cathedral.

Everything about it was in miniature, from the three tiny bedrooms to the long narrow sitting-room, well-equipped kitchen and gleaming bathroom. The owners were living abroad, the agent had told her.

Miranda sighed with pleasure and, once the removal van had departed, paused to take a breather and take stock of her surroundings. She stood in the middle of the sitting-room, dazed with happiness. This was home for the next few years, on an open-ended lease with a possible option to buy the freehold at some future date.

An impossible dream? No, if she saved like mad

from the generous salary she was receiving from the practice and added it to the modest nest egg she'd already accumulated she would be able to do it.

She closed her eyes, hugged herself and pirouetted around on the spot like a ballet dancer between the tea-chests that waited to be unpacked. And then she froze. . . Something cold and wet was brushing and snuffling against her bare ankles where the edge of her jeans didn't quite reach her trainers.

Slowly, taking a deep breath, she opened her eyes and looked cautiously down. A pair of liquid amber eyes gazed unwinkingly up at her out of a black and tan, shaggy, hairy doggy face with a rather distinguished long nose.

Miranda let out a breath and dropped to her knees. 'Oh, you beauty,' she said, stroking the silky ears. 'How did you get in?' The dog, which seemed to be a mixture of collie and something else, waved a feathery tail and looked innocent.

There was a ring at the doorbell. Miranda put her fingers through the dog's collar and led him across the room into the tiny hall. 'I bet this is someone looking for you,' she muttered.

The front door was partly open. She opened it wide.

Dr Brodie stood on the doorstep.

They stared at each other.

'You!' they said in unison.

Miranda's heart began to thump so hard that she thought he would hear it. She felt the blood come and go in her cheeks. She was surprised by the wave of pleasure that washed over her at the sight of him.

For a moment the doctor looked surprised and even, she thought, pleased to see her as a smile touched his mouth and his eyes. But the smile quickly disappeared.

'Sorry about Henry,' he said, indicating the dog and not sounding particularly sorry. 'The door was open—

which it shouldn't have been.' His voice was terse, and he frowned. 'This might not be Birmingham, but we do have occasional burglaries. An open door is an invitation. Henry thought it was—he's used to visiting here.'

'I must have left it ajar after the removal men went,' Miranda explained, feeling humble and apologetic. She continued to hang onto Henry's collar, her fingers refusing to let go. She searched round for something else to say. 'The people who lived here have gone abroad. I expect the agent could give you their address if you want it.'

'I have it. They're old neighbours. I knew the house had been let, but not to whom.'

He sounded annoyed and irritated, as if she were the last person who should have been allowed to rent it. 'Well, it's to me,' she replied defiantly, lifting her chin. What was she being apologetic about? This was her home.

'So I see, Miss Gibbs.' His lips quivered slightly at the corners and his eyes were curiously bright, sliding over her from top to toe.

Was he laughing at her, or was he angry? There no way of knowing. The set of that stern mouth, even with the quiver, could mean anything. She suddenly realised how ridiculous it was—the two of them standing in the doorway, she still holding the dog and he getting steadily drenched.

Pulling Henry with her, she stepped back into the hall. 'Do come in,' she said, and added in a rush, 'You're getting dreadfully wet. Can I offer you coffee or tea or something? I was just going to have a cup myself.'

She thought he would refuse and, without really understanding why, hoped that he wouldn't.

He didn't, just asked, 'Sure you're not too busy?'

She was, of course, but she shook her head.

'Thank you.' He stepped into the tiny hall, dwarfing it by his height and the breadth of his shoulders. His long white trench coat, looking vaguely military, dripped on the polished parquet floor.

'I think it would be a good idea,' he said, 'if I take this off before venturing into your sitting-room.'

'Please do.'

He shook it off in the porch, before hanging it on the elegant old-fashioned hall-stand just inside the front door.

Miranda released Henry, and led the way into the sitting-room.

Dr Brodie followed her in and looked round with interest.

'My word, you have worked hard getting it straight,' he said. 'And how well your own furniture fits in.' He cast an approving eye round the room, taking in the piecrust table and ladderback chairs in the corner, the sofa bed, the bookcases and a pair of shabby but comfortable armchairs at either side of the elegant steel fireplace.

'And what a handsome piece this is.' With long, sensitive fingers he stroked the delicate rosewood writing desk which fitted perfectly beneath the window overlooking the front garden.

'Yes, an heirloom passed on to me by my grandmother. I love it; always have, since I was a little girl.'

He nodded. 'Something to be cherished,' he said softly, his firm lips curving into an incredibly gentle smile. His hand continued to caress the polished wood.

'Yes,' whispered Miranda. She couldn't think of anything else to say. The softness of his voice, the movement of his hand, mesmerised her. She stood and stared at him. His dark brown eyes caught and held hers—or did hers catch his. . .? There was a moment's hushed silence when even the wind and rain stopped beating against the windows. Then Henry gave a snuffling bark and thumped his tail on the floor, demanding attention.

Miranda shivered, and dragged her eyes away from the doctor's.

The smile had gone from his face. He said curtly, 'You're cold. It's chilly in here; the central heating's not on. I'll light a fire. The Hubbards kept logs in the coal cellar outside.'

I should refuse and send him away, she thought, resenting the arrogant way he was taking charge, yet not wanting to see him go. Wondering why she didn't and despising herself. Whatever had happened to her intention to be just coolly friendly toward this man? What was happening to her?

She said breathlessly, trying to sound firm, 'I don't need a fire, thank you. It's only September.'

'But a cold and wet day, and you've been working hard,' he replied with an air of exasperated patience. 'What you need is a hot drink. You make the coffee, Miss Gibbs, and I'll make the fire.'

He couldn't wait to be gone, thought Miranda hours later as she lay awake in her comfortable bed under the sloping ceiling in her tiny bedroom. They had made polite, stilted conversation whilst they drank their coffee, and as soon as he'd swallowed his he and Henry had departed. She had watched them disappear into the gloom of mist and rain of late afternoon as the cathedral clock had chimed five.

Her lovely sitting-room, glowing in the firelight, had seemed empty after they had gone. She missed both man and beast, she thought ruefully.

It had been a strange, unreal sort of visit, brief and charged with a suppressed electricity that had almost surfaced during their eye contact. Or had that all been in her imagination when she thought she had seen something akin to tenderness in his eyes?

Tenderness! It was so unlikely that she must have imagined it. And what had her eyes told *him*? That she liked him; liked him too well; felt drawn to him, in spite of the fact that he'd not given her any encouragement?

How could she have given herself away so blatantly? She, cool, confident, self-contained Miranda Gibbs, who knew how to keep men at a distance. It didn't bear thinking about. Her cheeks burned and she pulled the duvet over her head. Tomorrow she would have to start working with him—tomorrow and for the foreseeable future.

Right, as from tomorrow she would be the detached, career-orientated Sister Gibbs, distantly friendly and nothing more.

On this thought she finally went to sleep.

Miranda spent her first couple of days at the practice centre familiarising herself with the routine, getting to know members of staff, making notes about possible changes and catching up with the mountain of paperwork that needed attention.

To her relief, tinged—she reluctantly admitted to herself—with disappointment, she saw very little of Dr Tom Brodie. He had a large list of patients and was either busy in surgery or out on visits.

It was on the third morning that she had a head-on clash with Liz Fuller. She was tackling the combined nurse-receptionist duty roster which, prior to her appointment, had operated in a rather casual fashion, vaguely organised by Pat Payne and Liz, when Liz appeared in her office.

She stood in the doorway, with her blue eyes sparkling and tossing her bush of magnificent black hair, and said without preamble, 'If you're doing the off-duty you can put me down for Tom's mother and toddler clinic, now that Dee Foster's going on maternity leave.'

Tom, not Dr Brodie, thought Miranda, and said mildly, 'Thanks for the offer, Liz, but you're already down to do your usual Well Woman clinic in the evening. I've given you the afternoon off.'

'I'll have the morning off and work through.'

'That's a long stretch and there's no need. I want you on in the morning to do bloods and so on, and the toddler clinic's covered.'

'Who's covering it?'

'I am. It's an ideal opportunity for me to take on a clinic that's going begging.'

Her eyes piercing like daggers, Liz snarled, 'It's an ideal opportunity for you to get your claws into Tom, but you're too late. He and I have something going, so you'd better back off, Gibbs. You've got my job—you're not going to get the most eligible bachelor in the practice too.'

So he was a bachelor. Miranda stared back at her furiously angry colleague, and with difficulty controlled her own temper. 'I'm a professional, Liz. I never mix work with personal matters. As far as I'm concerned, Dr Brodie is just another doctor. You're welcome to him as a man.' Not quite true, whispered a small voice in the back of her mind which she ignored. 'But what's all this about stealing your job? I don't understand.'

'Don't you?' ground out Liz. 'Well, it's simple. I applied for the post as nurse manager and would have got it if it hadn't been for you, looking like someone on the front of *Vogue*. You must have made suckers out of the men, especially the merry widower.'

'Who?'

'Val Thorpe. He's divorced, but calls himself a

widower and goes after anything in skirts; he'd give you his vote just because of the way you look.'

Miranda bit back a scathing reply and said quietly, 'My looks had nothing to do with it, Liz. I've got the job because I'm well qualified and experienced.'

'Oh, yeah,' said Liz contemptuously and, turning on her heel, left the office.

Feeling battered by the encounter and seething with repressed anger, Miranda sat for a moment staring into space then buzzed Tom Brodie's room number on the internal phone.

'Are you free?' she asked sharply when he answered, ignoring a little flutter of pleasure at the sound of his voice.

'Yes, at this moment.'

'May I see you?'

'Of course. Do come up.'

She climbed the shallow stairs two at a time, rapped smartly on the doctor's door and entered.

'You should have told me,' she snapped as soon as she was inside the room.

He looked faintly surprised. 'Told you what?'

'That Liz Fuller had applied for the post as nurse manager—so she's just informed me.'

He said levelly, 'Oh, that. You're angry. I don't blame you. We did intend telling you but Liz asked us not to say anything; reckoned she could cope better if whoever got the job didn't know that she had been in the running. It seemed a kindness, the least we could do since she had lost out. I'd no idea that she was going to tell you herself.'

'A kindness!' She couldn't keep the contempt out of her voice. How could a bunch of intelligent people have reached such a decision over such a sensitive matter? Because he, Dr Brodie, had persuaded them to save his precious Liz Fuller's face. It had to be that.

She said bitterly, 'And what about me coping, Doctor, or anyone else who'd been appointed? It's difficult enough building a disparate group of people, some of whom have only just started to work together, into a team without a resentful colleague.'

Outwardly calm but inwardly holding down a desire to wrap his arms round her and kiss her beautiful, angry mouth, his brown eyes surveyed her thoughtfully. 'And would it have helped, had you known in advance?'

She said honestly, 'I don't know. But you know it's said that being forewarned is to be forearmed. I might not have taken the job. . .or made her resignation a condition of accepting.'

'You wouldn't have done that,' he said with an absolute certainty which surprised her. 'You've too kind a heart, and you're far too intelligent. You would know what repercussions that might cause.'

She was pleased that he thought her intelligent—so often men couldn't get past the barrier of her beauty. She was grateful to him for seeing beyond that.

Her anger petered out. He was right. She wouldn't have had the heart to demand Liz Fuller's resignation, but she might have decided not to move to Combe Minster. But she was here now, and here she meant to stay. And, after all, this was part of her job—to resolve problems.

'You're probably right,' she said, raising a faint smile. 'It wouldn't have been a sensible thing to do. Bad for the practice and would have made me a lot of enemies.'

'Exactly. Instead of one, or maybe two with Pat Payne—she's close to Liz.'

And are you close to Liz? she wanted to ask. Did you want want her to get the job? Is that why you were so tough on me and perhaps all the other candidates? Had he wanted Liz to get the job? It explained his antagonism. Would she always have that possibility to contend with?

Well, she wasn't going to get an answer to that, not yet anyway. Perhaps at some future date all would be revealed, she thought wryly. 'Thanks for telling me about Pat,' she said. 'It explains her reaction to me, knowing she's a special friend of Liz's.'

'Would you like me to have a word with them—see if I can pour some oil onto troubled waters?'

'Good Lord, no,' Miranda said vehemently. 'It's the last thing that I want you to do.' She was surprised that he'd suggested it.

'Yes, I rather thought it might be, but I felt that I had to offer. If there's anything else that I can do to help, you must let me know.'

Miranda nodded. 'Will do, Dr Brodie, but I'll sort it out.'

'I'm sure you will,' he said, and added in a surprisingly mild voice, 'And it's Tom.'

'Tom,' she repeated, stilling a little flutter of pleasure as she said it. Was this a sort of olive branch he was offering—the gift of his name? He was staring at her hand, his eyes deep brown—almost black—pools. She wanted to say his name again. She moved her lips and murmured, '*Tom*,' on a whisper.

Tom couldn't take his eyes from her face. He loved the way she'd said his name in her slightly husky voice. To hell with being cool and distant. He didn't know whether he'd be able to. . .

The shrilling of the internal phone shattered his thoughts. He picked up the receiver, but as Miranda moved toward the door he motioned to her not to go. . . 'Yes?' he said sharply.

'Please come, Dr Brodie, pronto. There's a woman down here who looks as if she's about to give birth any minute, and I mean any minute.' It was Pat Payne, and she wasn't in the habit of panicking.

'Right, I'm on my way. Call an ambulance.' He slammed the phone down and gave Miranda a grim, ironic grin. 'Done any midwifery lately?' he asked as he stood up and crossed the room.

He took her arm and steered her, at a brisk pace, through the door and down the stairs, relaying Pat's message as they went. 'And if Pat says it's an emergency it is, so you'd better be ready for a bit of serious hands-on nursing. The ambulance might not get here on time.'

Everything about that birth bore the hallmarks of disaster. The woman, Julie Jones, was forty-two and it was a first baby. She was on holiday alone in Combe Minster; there wasn't a husband or partner or relative in sight. She was carrying a big baby which was overdue, and had been warned by her doctor not to go on holiday.

There had been some vague talk of a Caesarean because she had a smallish pelvis. She had ignored the early contractions that she'd experienced that morning, and taken herself for a walk. She was passing the surgery door when her waters broke, and had just managed to stagger into the building.

'Couldn't have chosen a better place,' she gasped through gritted teeth when Tom and Miranda arrived as she was having a contraction. 'I can feel it coming.'

Half carrying, half walking her, they managed—with help from Leigh Stewart, a junior partner who had arrived on the scene—to move her from Reception to the clinic room, where they heaved her onto the treatment couch.

Tom winked and gave her a wicked smile. 'You could have chosen the hospital,' he said. 'That would have been even better but, never fear, we can cope.'

His manner was warm, reassuring, friendly.

Miranda was impressed. Here was another side to Dr Tom Brodie. As Tom and Leigh performed a quick scrub at the clinic-room sink she peeled off the patient's wet trousers and panties, swabbed her vulva and thighs with antiseptic pads and draped a sheet over her updrawn knees and abdomen.

She began timing the contractions. They were coming fast. 'Take deep breaths and pant out, and don't push too hard,' she said quietly. 'Wait for the rhythm to take you.'

Tom pulled on a mask and disposable gloves from the sterile dressing trolley, folded back the sheet and did a quick internal examination. 'Fully dilated and crowning,' he said. 'Good. Now, another gentle push when you feel ready. I think this baby of yours is in a hurry.'

It was. The next few pushes, with Tom gently but firmly rotating the head through the canal, were followed soon afterwards by the shoulders and then the torso and legs of a perfectly formed baby.

There was a relieved expression on Tom's face as he held it up for the mother to see. His eyes were shining above his mask. 'You've a beautiful little girl, Julie,' he said softly.

Miranda took the baby from him, her eyes meeting his. She smiled at him and his eyes crinkled at the corners. She gave Julie the baby to hold for a moment. 'Give her a cuddle,' she murmured.

It had all taken an incredibly short time. Against the odds, the birth had been easy and natural, even leaving the perineum intact. A little later the placenta was safely delivered by Leigh. Miranda cleaned up the baby, wrapped her in a warm towel and then attended to Julie, making her clean and comfortable too with towels and couch sheets from the dressings cupboard.

The ambulance crew had arrived in the middle of proceedings, but there had been nothing for them to do except wait on events. Some half-hour later they were able to load mother and baby into the vehicle and drive them to the hospital.

All that could have gone wrong should have gone wrong in the circumstances, reflected Miranda, and it was a miracle that it hadn't.

'Every birth is a miracle,' said Tom when she voiced these thoughts aloud as they were sitting in the staff-room having a belated coffee. 'But I agree with you that this birth was, to say the least, a remarkable one, going against all the laws of medicine.'

'Yes, and it was such a beautiful baby.' Miranda smiled dreamily at the memory of the perfect little creature with a mop of black hair, miniature hands and feet and tiny red face screwed up with rage at being forced into the world.

Seeing the gentle smile flit across her lovely face and guessing in part at her thoughts, Tom wanted to reach out and touch her—stroke her cheek. She had looked marvellous holding the baby before handing it over to its mother.

The room was very quiet. There was a hushed, intimate quality between them. Surprising himself, he asked in a low voice, 'Do you want to have children, Miranda?'

It registered that he had called her Miranda in his deep throaty voice!

Did she want to have children?

She turned slowly to face him, the smile fading and her sea-green eyes becoming smoky and thoughtful. How to answer him, answer him honestly? Tell him that once she had dreamed, as most young women do, of meeting somebody special—of marrying and having a family—but the dream had faded? She hadn't met the somebody special, and she wouldn't settle for less.

Should she explain that most men wanted to treat her as an ornament, a sort of possession or a sex symbol without a mind of her own? That they didn't see her as a wife and mother but as someone to be shown off and admired—a tribute to their male ego. They didn't seem to be able to take aboard her kind of beauty and link it with domesticity.

No, of course she couldn't tell him anything of the sort. He wouldn't want to know, and she would embarrass him. He had sounded sincere but surely the question had been largely rhetorical, arising out of the unusual circumstances surrounding the birth of the Jones baby. He was probably already regretting that he had asked.

She said on a brittle laugh, 'That's a loaded question, Dr Brodie.'

He interjected, 'Tom.'

'Tom. Perhaps, one day. I'm not sure. At the moment I'm concentrating on my career; that's enough to be going on with. And the world's a pretty grim place to bring children into. . .wars, drugs, poverty, unemployment. . .'

'But these things have always been with us. The human race would have ground to a halt long ago if people had stopped having children on that account.'

'True, but I'm not sure that I could bear to see a child of mine put at risk. I'm not sure that it's the responsible thing to do. I'd want my child to have every chance.'

'But, supposing you were able to give it every chance, wouldn't you want to have a child then?' He was very persistent, his eyes bright and questioning as they looked hard into hers.

She took a deep breath and then said briskly, 'Yes, probably, if it was in partnership with the right person.'

'But of course,' he said gravely, his eyes brightening still further, 'that goes without saying.' He looked at his watch and stood up. 'I must be off. Visits before lunch. The usual daily grind goes on in spite of the advent of a new baby.'

Miranda stood up too. 'And I've a mound of the inevitable paperwork to finish.'

'That's never-ending,' he smiled. He turned away, but paused at the door. 'By the way, have you decided yet who is to take over my mother and toddler clinic?'

The question came out of the blue, a reminder that this was how the eventful morning had begun—with Liz attacking her over the clinic. She returned his smile. 'Yes—I am,' she said firmly, giving him a direct look and daring him to challenge her.

'I see.' His voice and eyes were suddenly expressionless. Was he disappointed or angry? She wasn't sure.

'Unless, of course, you'd prefer somebody else. . .' Her voice trailed off. Would he ask for Liz Fuller?

He shook his head slowly. 'No, I think not. I've no particular preference as to who's assisting me as long as it's someone capable, and you're certainly that, Sister Gibbs.'

So it was back to the formal 'Sister Gibbs' again. 'Thank you,' she said, her voice as expressionless as his.

He stared at her for a moment and then his mouth softened and he almost smiled. 'Well, I see no reason why we shouldn't make a super team if we work as well together in the future as we did this morning.'

'I'm sure we will, Dr Brodie,' she said steadily.

'Oh, I *do* hope so, Miranda,' he said in a low, fierce voice. 'I *do* hope so,' and with a nod he disappeared through the doorway into the corridor.

Miranda stood for a moment, staring at the space he had left, her mind in a whirl. He had sounded so vehement, as if he was willing them to work well together—very much wanted them to—but wasn't sure if they could.

Why should he behave so out of character—as if he were rattled by something over which he had no control? Was she responsible? Had she given herself away, let him see that she was attracted to him? Did he find that an embarrassment, especially with Liz Fuller around? Is that why he doubted if they could work together?

Hell, she hoped not. She was probably wildly wrong, but she would play it doubly cool in the future. Nothing was going to stop her making a success of this job; it was hers and she meant to keep it. Nobody, not even the charismatic Dr Brodie, was going to divert her.

On this resolution she made her way back to her office and got stuck into the paperwork piled on her desk.

CHAPTER FOUR

THE working week behind her, Miranda spent her first weekend in Almond Terrace pottering round her cottage and tiny garden. She polished furniture, weeded, trimmed unwieldy bushes and swept up leaves.

On Sunday morning she exchanged greetings with her neighbours, Sue and Andrew Palmer, and was invited for coffee.

'We own the sports shop in Market Square,' volunteered Sue over their coffee. 'What do you do, Miranda?'

'I've just started as nurse manager at the medical centre.'

'Ah, so you know Tom Brodie,' said Andrew. 'He's by way of being a neighbour—lives in The Pallant.'

'I knew he lived nearby.'

'Great guy—in our set at the social club. You should join. We've got everything—tennis and squash courts, pool, sauna.'

'Tom's a dish,' sighed Sue. 'Lucky you, working with him every day.'

'Not every day,' laughed Miranda. 'Sometimes our paths don't cross at all.' She looked at her watch. 'Heavens, I must go. Thanks for the coffee. You must come to me as soon as I get straightened out.'

'Look forward to it,' murmured Sue and Andrew in unison as they saw her out through the front door.

Nice couple, Miranda mused, letting herself into her own little house. Glad I've made contact with them. Funny how they both seem quite smitten with Tom Brodie.

She spent the afternoon unpacking books and pictures while listening to a Simply Red tape. In the early evening she phoned her sister, Juliet, in York.

'How are you?' she asked.

'Harassed,' said Juliet. 'Hugo's working, even though it's Sunday, Daisy and Ben are playing up like mad and Lucy's fretful. God, you're lucky, Miranda, being footloose and fancy free. What I wouldn't give to be in your shoes.'

'Well, you wouldn't give up Hugo and the kids, for a start. And don't moan about Hugo being busy. He's lucky—a lot of architects are barely making the grade these days.'

'All right, stop lecturing me. Now, how are you settling in in the wilds of Dorset? Met any interesting men yet? Knowing you, I bet you're already wowing the local talent and have lined up a string of dates.'

'I should be so lucky. I'm a hard-working career woman. I haven't had time to socialise so far, though I had coffee with my next-door neighbours today. Nice couple. Want me to join the social club. It's got everything apparently—state-of-the-art stuff.'

'Sounds great. I didn't think a little place like Combe Minster would run to anything as grand as that.'

'The city's not very big but it serves a lot of villages in the country round about, like the medical centre does.'

'Well, you seem to have landed yourself a super job in a super location, Miranda, but I wish you were a bit nearer. It would be nice to see you occasionally, and the kids would love it.' Juliet sounded wistful.

'I'll pop up soon; take a long weekend as soon as I get things organised at this end.'

'Promise?'

'Promise.' She could hear the children's raised voices in the background and the baby crying. 'I'd better let you off the hook. Sounds as if you're needed.'

'And how—who'd be a mother? Bye, Miranda.' The phone crashed down.

Well, I would, said a little voice firm and clear inside her head as she slowly replaced the receiver. I'd be a mother right now if. . .

Frozen, Miranda stared at the inert phone as if it had spoken. She gave a shaky little laugh and said out loud, 'Rubbish, you don't mean that, not right now. Some time in the future perhaps—you're a career woman, remember.'

Of course she was a dedicated career woman. No way did she want to change that for commitment to a husband, home and family—certainly not now, perhaps never. She'd suffered a momentary aberration, a slushy sentimental reaction to a tearful baby and childish voices and a sudden vivid picture of her sister's untidy, happy household.

But her commitment was firmly to a single life and the cathedral practice. And it was on this confident resolution that she poured herself a dry Martini, prepared an omelette for her supper and sat down to watch her favourite serial on television.

Much as she had enjoyed her weekend, by Monday morning she was happy to return to work. As if to underline what she had said to Sue about not working regularly with Tom, she saw very little of him over the next couple of days.

On the Wednesday of that second week Val Thorpe, the self-styled merry widower whom she had met at her interview, appeared in her office.

He had been on a sailing holiday when she'd started work the previous week. He was very brown, his fair hair bleached white. Not very tall, fit but inclined to be chubby, his handsome boyish face was wreathed in smiles and his hazel eyes twinkled as he bounced in.

'Well, hello there, Sister Gibbs,' he drawled. He paused dramatically. 'Or may I call you Miranda?' he asked in a throaty, sexy voice. He perched on a corner of the desk, leaned over and with a flourish offered her a darkly tanned hand to shake.

Miranda put her hand into his and wasn't surprised when he held it longer than necessary, only letting it go when she gave it a firm tug. He was such an obvious flirt that he was harmless, she decided.

Resisting a temptation to respond to his flirting by batting her eyelids, she smiled up at him. 'You may call me Miranda, Dr Thorpe,' she said, deliberately demure.

He grinned down at her. 'And you may call me anything you like, luscious lady,' he said with a chuckle, 'but my friends call me Val, and I would like you so much to be my friend—please?' His teasing eyes were full of admiration. He lifted her hand from the desk and held it as if it were something precious.

Miranda fought down a desire to giggle. He was being deliberately over the top, but Liz Fuller was probably right—he would get carried away by a pretty face and, given the least encouragement, easily misread any interest she might show in him.

She must lay down the ground rules—her rules—immediately. 'Friends,' she said firmly, 'just friends. Understood, Val?' She looked him straight in the eye.

'You're warning me off. . .' He didn't finish the sentence but knew that she really meant what she'd said, and was telling him that anything more than friendship was definitely not on.

Miranda nodded. 'That's right.'

He gave a theatrical sigh. 'You're a hard lady, Miranda, but, yes, understood—just friends. Any little crumb gratefully received.' With an exaggerated gesture, he raised her hand to his lips and kissed her fingertips.

'You're incorrigible,' laughed Miranda.

There was a knock at the half-open door and it was pushed wide.

Tom Brodie stood in the doorway—tall, dark, lean, immaculate in a formal dark suit, cream silk shirt and mutedly patterned tie.

Miranda pulled her hand from Val's and felt a wave of colour hit her cheeks. Damn the man, he would appear now. She felt at a disadvantage and guilty, which was ridiculous as she had nothing to feel guilty about.

Rallying, she said in a bright, cool voice, 'Dr Brodie—Tom—do come in.'

Brodie stared silently at the tableau in front of him for a moment as expressions of disbelief and then distaste flickered across his face. 'I won't, thank you.' His upper lip curled contemptuously. 'My business can wait. I can see that yours can't.'

Surprised by the scarcely concealed disgust in his voice, Miranda looked at him in astonishment. Was he really so angry about a little bit of obvious flirting between two mature adults?

Val said cheerfully, 'Oh, don't be so bloody sarcastic, Tom, it's not like you. For heaven's sake, lighten up, man, we were just having a bit of fun. As a colleague, I'm simply welcoming Miranda to Combe Minster. You know—' he winked '—a Val Thorpe special welcome.'

Tom grated, 'Oh, I know only too well, Val, about the special sort of welcome that you've got in mind. I'll leave you to it, but don't forget that you've got a waiting-room full of patients,' and, turning on his heel, he marched off down the corridor.

Sarcastic, arrogant man, thought Miranda, wishing with all her heart that he hadn't caught her acting the coquette with Val, however innocently.

Val said in a surprised voice, 'Well, fancy Tom blowing his top like that. He knows that I have a weakness for beautiful women but that it never interferes with my work and I'm really quite harmless.' He shrugged and grinned.

'Perhaps,' said Miranda wryly as, remembering that Steven had once accused her of using her beauty to lead men on against their will, another possibility struck her, 'he doesn't think *I'm* quite harmless.'

'Afraid for *my* honour!' Val snorted with laughter. 'Well, I'm ready to risk it, lovely Miranda, if you are. Now, what about an intimate little dinner for two on Saturday night? Just a friendly dinner, no strings. I know of a nice place out of town.'

'I'll think about going out,' promised Miranda, 'but not an intimate little dinner—something more robust, like a pint and a pie at your local. Now go away and let me get on. Liz Fuller and Pat Payne are due any minute for a meeting.'

Val pulled a face and, suddenly serious, said thoughtfully, 'Having trouble with those two? Are they bitching things up for you?'

'They're being a bit difficult at the moment, but it's nothing that I can't handle. We'll work something out. After all, we're all professionals and have the good of the practice at heart.'

'Just watch your back,' advised Val. 'It's not only work we're talking about but. . . Oh, well, least said soonest mended, as my old granny used to say. But, remember, I'm always around if you need me. You know, white knight to the rescue and all that.'

He slid off the desk, crossed to the door, blew her a kiss and was gone, pulling the door to behind him.

There's more to that man than just an outrageous flirt, thought Miranda. There's a kind and serious person beneath the veneer. I just hope he doesn't get hurt playing the romantic fool.

And there's more to Tom Brodie, too, but I don't know what it is, she mused. Why had he blown hot and cold with her ever since she had arrived in Combe Minster? Why had he been so angry at finding her and Val Thorpe together? It didn't make sense. His brown eyes had blazed for a moment. If looks could have killed. . .

Surely it was obvious that they were just flirting harmlessly. Or did he really think that she was out to ensnare his colleague? And, if he did, why should that matter to him as long as their work wasn't affected?

Well, there was no question of that. She enjoyed socialising but she knew how to work hard as well as play hard, as the arrogant Dr Brodie would learn. He would have no cause to regret that she, Miranda Gibbs, had joined the cathedral practice. She would be a model nurse manager, impersonally professional and friendly at all times.

Impersonal and friendly! She had already decided to be that before coming to Combe Minster, but she was finding it increasingly difficult where Tom Brodie was concerned. Against her will, she found that he intrigued and attracted her in spite of his dislike of her.

Yet there had been no dislike when their eyes had met over baby Jones. That had been a special moment, with no room for anything but joy, and it had been reflected in his eyes.

Had she given herself away then? Let him see that she. . .she what? That she liked him; wanted him to like her; wanted his respect. Well, she wouldn't give herself away again. She would be on her guard from now on.

On guard against the charismatic Tom Brodie! It was

ridiculous, but she didn't want to be; she wished it was otherwise.

A curious tremor of pain ran through her and her heart felt as if it were being squeezed. She frowned and took a deep breath. From now on Tom Brodie was definitely off limits, except where work was concerned. A no-go area, she thought sadly, that she must avoid at all costs, for her own good and that of the practice.

The good of the practice! What about Liz Fuller—how to deal with her? It would be necessary to convince that resentful lady that she, Miranda, had absolutely no personal interest in Tom Brodie, and in that way win over her support in the management of the medical centre.

What would she do if that didn't work? Take a tough stand, imply that her job would be on the line if she didn't co-operate? Not clever. A desperate measure to take and one that would certainly be resisted by Dr Brodie and alienate other staff. But what option would she have if she was to retain her authority? Resign herself?

No, that would be a cop-out—an admission of defeat. She just had to hope that Liz would see sense and toe the line and, if she did, that Pat Payne would follow suit. She needed the goodwill of both these women if the practice was to run smoothly.

With a sigh Miranda stood up, crossed to the window and gazed out across the square to the cathedral, basking in the mellow September sunshine. She would call in there on her way home tonight, perhaps catch Evensong. But even if she didn't it would be soothing and comforting to visit the ancient building steeped in history and incense and prayer, and say a private prayer of her own.

But she had the rest of the day to get through before she could do that, starting with the interview with Liz and Pat which she was dreading but which had to be faced. And when, a moment later, there was a knock at the door she squashed her fears, squared her shoulders and called out a brisk, 'Come in.'

In the event, it didn't go off too badly. Though both women entered the office looking stony-faced, they perhaps sensed Miranda's determination not to stand any nonsense and thawed somewhat when she offered them coffee, making it plain that this was meant to be a friendly meeting.

To her relief, they became quite animated over the new procedures that she suggested about both nursing and reception staff signing in when they came on duty. That's what she wanted—their input, even if she didn't agree with it, not the implacable indifference which had met her over the last few days.

'We never have signed on,' said Pat forcefully. 'Don't like the idea of being kept track of, as if we worked in a factory. My staff don't need tabs kept on them.'

'And that goes for the nursing staff too,' said Liz. 'They can all be trusted.'

'It's not a question of trust,' explained Miranda. 'It's so that it can been seen at a glance who's on duty and covering duties as charted. After all, there can be a lot of receptionists on at any one time and they're not always in the front office, nor do they always come on at the same time.'

'The same applies to the nurses. We need to know that they're here, and if they're not do something about it promptly.'

'But we always manage to sort things out eventually,' said Pat indignantly.

'And lose time because you don't know if somebody's in or not for perhaps ten, twenty minutes,' retorted Miranda. 'Let's give it a whirl. And it will help us find if we've got our staffing levels right; decide if we need more people on at certain times of the day. Plan the duty roster better to cover each day's individual requirements.'

'Is this a cost-cutting exercise?' asked Liz suspiciously.

'Not at all.' Miranda was emphatic. 'In fact, we might want more staff as more specialists are engaged to do clinics. As you know, the partnership aims to have a range of ancillary health care services attached to the practice—everyone from a massage therapist to a visiting psychiatrist. The emphasis is on patient care and keeping our patients off the hospital waiting-lists, but we do have to justify expenses to the accountants and we can best do this by being efficient.'

'Accountants!' scoffed Pat. 'What do they know?'

'Not a lot about running a super health practice,' agreed Miranda, 'which is why we've got to be specific about our needs. But the doctors will have the last word, and they'll back us all the way if we convince them that any changes we want to make are worthwhile. This is a fair-sized practice, running on a substantial budget, not several small ones running on a shoestring. Together the three of us can make this place work. You're super at your jobs, and I know mine. Let's bury our differences for the good of the practice. We don't want to let patients or doctors down.'

Liz gave Miranda a hard, straight, challenging look that spoke volumes. 'For the good of the practice,' she said, raising her coffee-mug as if proposing a toast. 'And I won't let anyone down, least of all the doctors.'

Pat lifted her mug. 'And I second that,' she murmured. 'To the doctors and the practice.'

'Good,' said Miranda briskly, to hide her relief. 'I'm glad we're agreed. Now, there are a few more points that I'd like to raise and get feedback on.'

The meeting went on for another twenty minutes before Miranda brought it to an end. 'We'll meet again in a day or two,' she said as Liz and Pat were leaving, 'and thrash out any more problems. Please keep the ideas rolling in. Suggestions from both staff and patients are welcome. And, Pat, give some thought to the storing of medical records along the lines we've discussed.'

'Will do,' said Pat, who was actually looking pleased as she left the office.

But Liz frowned and hesitated in the doorway. 'Did you mean it,' she asked abruptly, 'what you said the other day about not being in any way interested in Tom Brodie, except as a doctor?'

Miranda clenched her fists beneath the desk and took a deep breath. 'Of course I meant it,' she said firmly. 'I'm a career woman. Work comes first with me. I like an occasional date, but I'm not in the habit of pinching other people's partners. I promise you, Liz, as far as I'm concerned Dr Brodie is all yours.'

'Oh, he is,' said Liz. 'You'd better believe it.' And, with a triumphant smile, she followed her friend down the corridor.

Miranda was busy for the rest of the day, and had no time to dwell on Liz's parting shot or Tom's curious reaction to her and Val earlier.

She had a working sandwich lunch in the staffroom with Kay Brent and Lydia Woods, discussing future plans for the practice. Both doctors were full of ideas, and keen on extending facilities to qualified practitioners specialising in alternative medicine such as hypnotherapy and acupuncture to treat long-term pain and depression.

They also wanted to set up their own family planning clinic now that the only one in the town had been closed down through lack of funds. They thought there might be some opposition from the other partners, particularly in relation to the alternative medicine project. Could they count on her support at the senior staff meeting? they wanted to know.

'Well, in principle, yes,' she said, 'but I'd like to hear the argument for and against before committing myself. They're both big projects that would have to prove viable.'

'Sitting on the fence,' gibed Kay good-humouredly.

'No,' retorted Miranda, 'trying to be sensible, be a good manager and think what's best for the practice—which means for the patients.'

By two o'clock Miranda was on duty in the surgery, taking the general clinic, and there were already a number of people waiting to see her.

Her first patient, a Mrs Sweet, had come for the removal of stitches from a small wound on her neck from which a tiny cyst had been removed and sent for biopsy. She was a nervous, thin lady of sixty. Her fingers were so shaky that Miranda had to unbutton her blouse for her.

'Relax, Mrs Sweet, it's not going to hurt,' said Miranda, giving her a reassuring smile.

'Oh, I'm not afraid of it hurting,' whispered Mrs Sweet, 'but I'm so afraid that I might have cancer, though Dr Brodie—when he took the lump out—said that he thought it was just a simple cyst. I asked at the desk but the results of the test haven't come back yet, and I can't help thinking that's a bad sign.'

'No, it isn't,' explained Miranda firmly. 'The hospital does dozens of biopsies every week and they do them quickly, but getting the results out to the doctors takes time. But, anyway, if Dr Brodie thought that the cyst was benign I'm sure you have nothing to worry about. He's a super doctor.'

'Oh, he's lovely,' agreed Mrs Sweet, with a sigh. 'So reassuring. He said that even if there is anything wrong we've caught it early, and there are lots of things that can be done about it.'

'Then stop worrying, love,' Miranda said gently. 'Now, let's get these stitches out.'

The next two patients on the list were a middle-aged husband and wife, going on a trek across Africa, who needed immunisation against cholera, typhoid and yellow fever, among other things. Miranda suggested that these injections and inoculations be spread out over several weeks, and booked the couple in for several more sessions.

'I'll give you the typhoid injection today,' she explained, 'since this will have to be repeated, and can cause localised pain and inflammation for a couple of days. It will give you time to get over it before the top-up one's due. Next week the cholera vac, which will last about six months, and lastly the yellow fever one, which should last for about ten years.'

'Go on, then, Sister, do your worst,' said Mr Robbins, pulling a face as he rolled up his shirtsleeve, displaying a hairy, muscular arm. 'I've had most of these before when I was in the army.'

'Isn't he the brave one, then?' said Mrs Robbins with a wide grin. 'But at least he doesn't faint at the sight of a needle, like some tough men do.'

'Oh, he's very brave,' laughed Miranda as she prepared the injection.

Their injections given, the Robbins departed happily hand in hand. Obviously on the same wavelength, a loving and devoted couple, thought Miranda as she called in the next patient.

Mrs Frost had been seen by the general surgery nurse

two weeks previously for treatment of an extensive varicose ulcer on her leg.

'You were booked to come in last week, Mrs Frost, to have the dressing on your leg changed, but you didn't. What happened?' Miranda asked.

Mrs Frost looked half apologetic, half truculent. 'My family arrived unexpectedly and I couldn't make it. I phoned and explained to the receptionist. She said it would be all right to come this week.'

Miranda sighed silently. This was something that she'd have to take up with both Liz and Pat; receptionists must just not go around making this sort of judgement, and the nurse on duty should have followed the missed appointment through.

'But you knew that it was important that the dressing was changed last week, Mrs Frost. If you'd spoken to the nurse she would have arranged to see you the next day.'

'Well, that's not what the receptionist said.' Mrs Frost looked scared. 'Has it made it worse, not being looked at?'

'I'll know that when I've removed this dressing,' said Miranda gently as she began to unwind the covering bandage.

As she had feared, the dressing pad was adhered to the ulcerated area by a smelly pus- and blood-stained exudate and took a long time to ease off with antiseptic cleansing swabs. For all the care she took, it was a painful process and Mrs Frost looked quite distressed by the time she had finished. Miranda gave her a glass of water, which she sipped gratefully.

'How is it?' she asked in a trembly voice.

'Not good, I'm afraid,' replied Miranda, looking grimly at the pus-filled area fringed with necrotic tissue. 'I'm going to have to get the on-call doctor to have a look at it.'

The on-call doctor *would* be Tom Brodie, she thought ruefully.

'I won't have to go into hospital, will I?'

'Most unlikely, I should think, but let's wait and see what Dr Brodie has to say. He certainly won't send you into hospital unless it's absolutely necessary, but he may want you to see a specialist. I'll just give him a ring and put him in the picture.'

She rang his consulting-room.

'I'll be down shortly, Sister,' he said in reply to her rather guarded call from the surgery.

He sounded stiff and formal but, then, she had been stiff and formal too. What else could they be with each other after this morning's little contretemps? Her heart beat fractionally faster as she put down the phone. She had hoped to put off coming face to face with him so soon, but work had dictated otherwise. But at least she had the protection of a patient's presence, ensuring that they both behaved professionally.

She made small talk with Mrs Frost while they waited for Tom to appear, and when he arrived a few minutes later she was her usual cool, composed self.

He was cool and composed too, giving the patient and Miranda a wide smile that crinkled up the corners of his eyes. As if nothing had happened, thought Miranda with a spurt of annoyance. Though quite how she thought he might have behaved, she wasn't sure.

'Sister tells me that we've got a problem with this ulcer of yours,' he said to Mrs Frost, his manner kind and unhurried. 'Let's have a look at it.' He put on his horn-rimmed spectacles and bent over her exposed leg to peer at the wound intently. With gentle fingers he tested the inflamed but intact skin round the wound.

'Hmm, messy, could break down further,' he muttered. He looked up over the rim of his specs at Miranda, his eyes grave. 'As you say, a lot of necrotic tissue. If we can clear that we're on our way, and if not. . . What have we used so far?'

Miranda reeled off the various treatments that had been tried.

'Right, then let's try Intrasite gel. Have we got any to hand?'

Miranda checked the dressings cupboard and found the mushroom-like dispenser containing the gel. 'Yes,' she confirmed.

'Then I suggest we clean up the wound with that, cover it with a paraffin gauze dressing and keep it in place with a firm support bandage. With luck, that'll do the trick and we'll have a nice clean ulcer that will begin healing. If it doesn't work we'll have to have another think.'

He smiled down at the patient and put a hand on her shoulder. 'Right, Mrs Frost, Sister will see to this for you and make you much more comfortable. But I want you to rest that leg as much as possible, raise it on a pillow when you're on your bed—give it a chance to heal. Take soluble aspirin or paracetamol tablets at night if it's giving you pain, and promise me you'll come back in a week's time for a check-up—or earlier if you're worried about it.'

'Oh, I will, Doctor. I'll never miss an appointment again, I promise; I've learnt my lesson.'

He beamed at her. 'Good, never too late to learn. We'll see you here next week, then. Now, I'm just going to borrow Sister for a minute or two.' He switched his glance from her to Miranda. 'Sister, a word, if you please.' Very professional, very proper. He crossed to the door and held it open.

With a little prickle of apprehension running down her spine, Miranda slipped past him into the empty corridor. What on earth could he have to say to her? Would it have anything to do with her flirting with

Val? Surely not. He wouldn't pursue anything so trivial unless, of course, he didn't consider it trivial.

Tom closed the surgery door firmly behind him, leant against it and stood, looking down at the flower-like face tilted up to his. Tendrils of shining honey-blonde hair curled against her lightly bronzed cheeks. He longed to touch it. Her clear green eyes met his steadily and frankly. God, she was beautiful.

Did she have the faintest idea what her beauty could do to a man, especially a man like Val Thorpe, who was divorced, lonely, vulnerable? Or did she know only too well, and use her beauty deliberately as a weapon, a trap?

No! He couldn't believe that of her; didn't want to believe it. But he had a duty, not only to Val but to the practice.

His heart lurched against his ribcage. Better get on with it. He cleared his throat, but his voice still came out as a husky baritone.

He said bluntly, dismayed at his own bluntness and lack of finesse which normally came so naturally to him, 'We have to talk, but not here—somewhere where we won't be disturbed. What time are you off duty?'

'About six, but. . .'

'I'll be off soon after when surgery's finished. I suggest we meet in The Cellary wine bar for a drink.'

He suggested! The nerve of the man. His eyes were dark, hard, piercing, almost daring her to refuse. She kept hers fixed unwaveringly on his. She would *not*, *not* look away as if she had something to hide.

Her voice steady, she asked, 'Wouldn't your consulting-room or my office be just as convenient for a talk concerning practice affairs?'

'This isn't just practice business—there's a personal angle. And, if we're on the spot, we're bound to bc interrupted by the odd phone call and so on—we're too available.' His eyes softened a little and he added, in a low, insistent voice, 'Do come, Miranda. It's important to both of us and to the practice.'

He pushed himself away from the door and, for a moment, Miranda thought he was going to touch her. She caught her breath and moved back a step. What personal angle? There was nothing personal between them to discuss, unless there was something that she didn't know about—something that would explain his dislike of her from day one. But what that could be, she hadn't a clue.

She had to know. She had to meet him, even if it broke all the promises she had made to herself about being wholly and only professional with him. And he had asked her politely enough, with no sign of arrogance. It would be churlish to refuse. He was a colleague.

What harm could it possibly do—a single meeting in a crowded bar? Liz Fuller popped into her head. Forget Liz Fuller—this had nothing to do with her relationship with Tom. For, in spite of any personal angle involved, this was more a business meeting than anything, for the good of the practice, and she would treat it as such. She had nothing to feel guilty about. The thought cheered her.

'All right, the wine bar, six-fifteen or thereabouts,' she said brightly. 'Now I must get back to Mrs Frost.' Flashing him a smile, she slid past him and whisked back into the clinic room.

Tom stared at the closed door for a few moments, savouring her smile and quietly exulting in the knowledge that he had persuaded her to meet him. The thought of spending an hour in her company, even though it might be an uncomfortable one, was as exhilarating as a shot of adrenalin.

He had acted on impulse, but the idea that they might

talk had been hovering round in the back of his mind ever since this morning's unpleasant little episode. The desire to put things right with Miranda, to offer some sort of explanation for his over-the-top reaction to finding her flirting with Val, was intense.

What sort of explanation? Hardly the plain, unvarnished truth. That he had been stunned from the moment he'd clapped eyes on her—by her beauty, by the intelligence that shone out of her lovely face—and that seeing her making up to Val had sent shock waves of jealousy shafting through him. The kind of searing jealousy to which he had thought himself immune since a young man.

For one mad, ecstatic moment he thought of doing just that—being totally honest with her and laying his heart at her feet.

Hell, not possible. She, the fiercely independent career woman, would think him crackers. He thought himself crackers that he, cool, sophisticated Tom Brodie, should succumb like a schoolboy. No way could he let her see the devastating effect she was having on him.

So, what should he tell her? Half the truth, of course. Hand on heart, he could explain that he was genuinely concerned for Val—for his vulnerability. Make her understand that beneath the lightweight exterior there lurked a sensitive man who might easily be hurt. Surely this lovely clever woman would respond to that sort of plea? For it was in her nature to be gentle and understanding as a nurse, though by some magic she managed to combine this with being a detached, efficient manager too.

He had completely misjudged her when he'd thought her a calculating *femme fatale*. She was nothing of the sort. How could he have been so wrong? He was disgusted with himself. She didn't flaunt her beauty or her seniority; she was already blending into the practice, and the staff were beginning to accept her as one of themselves. She was going to be an asset, not the liability that he had feared.

Somehow, without revealing the true state of his feelings, he had to get this over to Miranda—clear the air between them, start off on a new footing and establish a friendly working relationship. He had put up barriers from the beginning; it was up to him to pull them down.

Well, tonight he would make a beginning and let her see that he valued her as a colleague. Valued her as a colleague! That was an understatement. He valued her, full stop—and perhaps at some future date he might tell her so. But that, he thought wryly as he made his way to his room, was in the lap of the gods.

Miranda was run off her feet for the rest of the afternoon to catch up with patients who were booked in every fifteen minutes or so, having been delayed because of the time it had taken to deal with Mrs Frost. But they were all quite straightforward cases—several more injections, an ear that needed syringing, a couple of cervical smears, another couple of dressings—nothing for which she had to call on Dr Brodie again for advice or instruction.

It was nearly six by the time she had finished her list, made up her notes, dealt with the various instruments she had used and generally tidied the clinic room.

Back in her office, she pondered over Tom's pressing request for a meeting. Strange that he wanted to see her and talk to her after the unpleasant little incident this morning. Was he regretting his action then? Did he realise that he had jumped to the wrong conclusion about her and Val? Nothing in his manner had indicated that. He had been simply polite and insistent that they meet.

They were to meet soon! Her heart gave a little uncontrollable jerk at the prospect. 'Stop it,' she muttered. 'Get a hold of yourself.'

But the admonition didn't work. Her heart continued to pound uncomfortably at the thought of sharing a drink with Tom Brodie in a kind of no man's land, unprotected by the cloak of professionalism. With a strange feeling that life was spiralling out of her control, she changed out of uniform into the jeans, sweater and chunky knit jacket she had worn to work that morning.

A few minutes later, bidding goodnight to the receptionists on duty, she made her way out through the still-busy waiting-room—where patients waited to see the doctors holding late surgeries—and into the square.

CHAPTER FIVE

IT WAS a chilly evening, though the September sun was still shining low in the sky and casting long shadows across the square in front of the cathedral.

Miranda shivered with cold and in anticipation of her meeting with Tom Brodie. She buttoned her thick navy-blue knit jacket more closely round her and turned up the wide collar, glad of its warmth but fleetingly wishing that it was rather more stylish.

Not that it mattered. He wouldn't notice or care what she wore. A frisson of annoyance—sadness—regret—rippled through her.

She wasn't sure which emotion was uppermost. Neither was she sure why she was so drawn to this aloof, enigmatic man. Was it because he, unlike most men, seemed impervious to her beauty? Well, that made it a refreshing and even, she acknowledged honestly, a challenging change.

Not that she wanted to challenge him, exactly. But it was ironic, she thought sadly, that this man whose approval was important to her had disliked her from the time of their first meeting. But, in spite of his instant dislike, he had fascinated her, drawn her like a magnet—though he had seldom been more than politely courteous.

He had unbent on the day that Julie Jones had so dramatically and miraculously given birth to her baby. But the atmosphere then had been special, charged with emotion. They had worked smoothly and in harmony together to help a new scrap of humanity into the world, and, because of it, he had momentarily warmed toward her.

But in the days following he had kept his distance, been correct and professional as before and nothing more. At least until this afternoon. And now, suddenly, he wanted to meet her, talk to her—had almost pleaded with her to do so. She wished that she knew why.

Her imagination ran riot. As far as she could tell, though he wanted to talk to her it was as though he felt compelled to do so against his will. Perhaps he was going to ask for her resignation and wanted to do it discreetly, away from the practice premises! Perhaps Liz Fuller had persuaded him, in spite of her apparent co-operation that morning, that she, Miranda, wasn't right for the practice!

No, with absolute certainty she knew that he wouldn't allow himself to be influenced so easily, not even by the woman he loved. He might regret her appointment as nurse manager, but he would play fair and give her every opportunity to prove herself—of that she was confident. He might be stiff and stand-offish with her, but he was a man of integrity.

The Cellary wine bar was tucked away in the shadow of the cathedral. It was exactly what its name implied—a vast, low-ceilinged cellar with massive pillars and arches supporting the roof, burrowing under a medieval building housing solicitors' offices and an estate office. Called a wine bar, it was, in fact, licensed to sell beer and spirits too.

It was crowded at this hour with people calling in for drinks on their way home from work. Miranda paused just inside the door near the top of the spiral staircase to look down on the sea of heads below, searching for an empty table.

Somebody crowded through the door behind her. She

felt a hand pressing in the small of her back.

'Do you mind?' she said sharply, pushing away the hand. She turned to glare indignantly over her shoulder, and found herself staring straight into Tom Brodie's dark brown eyes.

'Sorry,' he said softly, 'I was just about to speak; let you know I was here. I didn't mean to frighten you.'

Miranda drew in a quick breath. 'You didn't *frighten* me.' Her voice was scathing. 'I just thought you were someone getting fresh. You're lucky that I didn't stamp on your toes.'

His eyebrows shot up and his eyes gleamed. 'Is that your first line of defence?'

'Always,' she said firmly, though she allowed her lips to curve into a smile. 'Act first, talk later—big city manners.'

His mouth twitched at the corners. 'Very sensible, too, even in Combe Minster.' The street door opened behind him and somebody else joined them on the platform. 'We'd better move,' he said. 'Look, there's a table over there by the fireplace. You grab it and I'll get the drinks. What'll you have?'

'A very dry vermouth with ice and lemon, please.'

'Right.'

Miranda wove her way round the crowded tables to the pew-like oak settle nestling in the inglenook by the massive stone fireplace, where monster logs glowed like jewels. She sniffed—wood smoke, nice. She gazed dreamily into the crimson red heart of the fire.

What could Tom Brodie have to say to her that he couldn't or wouldn't discuss on the practice premises? she asked herself yet again. Why this sort of semi-secrecy? Not that a crowded bar could be termed a secret rendezvous—in fact, quite the opposite. He certainly didn't mind if they were seen together; had simply insisted that they had their chat on neutral ground.

At least it shouldn't be an acrimonious discussion. They had broken the ice by meeting at the top of the stairs, she mused, feeling oddly comforted by the thought.

She was jerked out of her reverie by Tom, arriving with the drinks. He set them down on the table and sat down on the narrow settle beside her. He slanted a sideways look at her and said quietly, 'Thanks for coming, Miranda; I appreciate it.' She was conscious of his lean but muscular thigh almost touching hers, and could feel the heat pulsing from it.

Her heart thudded uncomfortably at his closeness. Ridiculous! She, unnerved by a man! Why *was* she so rattled? She scrunched herself into the corner of the settle and, to avoid looking at him, picked up her glass and took a sip of wine.

'I could hardly refuse, could I?' she asked lightly. 'You were so insistent—but I can't think what we've got to talk about that isn't strictly business.'

'It's awkward; it's about Val Thorpe.' He saw the look of distaste that flitted across Miranda's face and added quickly, 'Nothing malicious, I assure you. Not just empty gossip.'

Partly reassured, she asked, 'What about him?'

'He's not quite what he seems, you know. I wouldn't like him to get hurt.'

'And you think I might hurt him?'

Tom took a deep breath and a mouthful of lager, and nodded. 'Yes, inadvertently, I think you might.'

Miranda frowned. 'Because you found us harmlessly chatting each other up this morning? Two mature, sophisticated adults. Really, you've got to be joking.'

He shook his head slowly and picked his words with care. 'No, not because of that, but because you are an astonishingly beautiful woman and Val's particularly vulnerable—you may not realise how vulnerable. It's an act, you know, that he puts on, pretending to be this devil-may-care lady's man. Beneath the veneer he's... well, he's a different person. I'm afraid that he might have read more into your willingness to exchange sexy innuendos with him than you can imagine.'

'I know,' said Miranda evenly. 'I'd already sussed that out, and laid down a few ground rules. I think we understand each other well enough; he knows exactly where he stands with me. But, even if he doesn't, I can't see what it's got to do with you, Dr Brodie. You're not his keeper.'

'No, but I am his closest friend; we've been friends for years. I was his best man at his wedding and I worry about him. You know, I presume, that he was married and is divorced, not widowed—the self-styled merry widower is a cover-up, especially the merry bit.'

'I knew that he was divorced, but not why he calls himself the merry widower.'

'Because,' said Tom heavily, 'it's easier for him to pretend to be happy and carefree—a merry widower or gay divorcee. Because he's never got over losing his wife. To him, when she walked out and left him, it was as if she'd died. For a few months he went to pieces entirely—nearly drank himself to death.'

He paused and took another mouthful of lager.

'Then quite suddenly he seemed to come to terms with the divorce, invented this new persona for himself and began living up to it. And it's worked, up to a point, in a fragile sort of way. He's been coping fine for the last few years—a few lightweight affairs, nothing serious; nobody's got hurt.'

'But now you think I might hurt him. Why should I, for heaven's sake?'

He was silent for a moment and looked down into

his drink, knowing that his eyes would be a dead give-away, then said crisply with a shrug of his broad shoulders, 'Quite simply because you're so stunning, Miranda. Flawlessly beautiful, just like his ex-wife—too like his ex-wife, except that her beauty was superficial. Though Val couldn't see that until they parted. But you have those qualities that he admires—qualities that he thought he saw in her.'

'But he knows nothing about me or my qualities. He only met me at my interview and again today. We haven't even worked together yet.'

'He knows from your CV that you're a brilliant nurse manager and—by implication, and what was said at your references, and how you showed up at your interview—that you're a caring person.' With deliberate movements Tom set down his drink and, in the cramped pew, turned to face her. His leg touched hers and settled against it, warm, throbbing.

She wanted to move away, but couldn't. She tensed, quivered, held her breath, slowly turned her head and found herself staring into the depths of his velvet brown eyes—eyes full of. . . For a moment the bar noises floated away into nothingness and the space round them was silent.

Then Tom's voice, warm, rich and deep, broke the silence and sounds began to drift back. 'Oh, Miranda, love, don't you see? Just because you are you, you pose a threat to Val.'

He had called her 'love', this man who disliked her. She blinked, unlocking her eyes from his, and with an amazingly steady hand picked up her glass and took a sip of wine.

He hadn't meant anything by it, of course. It was just a figure of speech, a common impersonal endearment used by a lot of doctors and nurses to reassure. And, anyway, if anyone was his love in the truest sense of the word it was Liz Fuller—she had made that quite clear.

She dragged up a cool little smile, convincing herself that his eyes had lied moments before and that he didn't care a fig for her.

'And what,' she asked, 'am I supposed to do about that? Dye my hair; change my personality; pack up my bags and leave? Is that what you want, Dr Brodie—for me to leave your precious practice and make it safe for Val? Whatever you might think, I'm not a predatory female. I'm a career woman first and last.' Try as she might, she couldn't keep an edge of bitter sadness out of her voice—sadness that he should think so badly of her.

Tom swore beneath his breath. This was the last thing he wanted—to hurt her, his lovely Miranda, even to save Val being hurt. He ached to do the impossible—to take her in his arms and tell her that he loved her. That was out of the question, but how the hell was he going to put things right without giving himself away completely and letting her see how absolutely besotted he was with her?

Try being halfway honest, mocked a little voice in his mind. At least let her know that you appreciate what she is doing for the practice—that won't compromise you.

He said briskly, 'Don't even think about leaving, Miranda. You must know we're all impressed with how you are managing the practice so far—introducing small improvements, coming up with new ideas and winning over most of the staff in so short a while. Don't think that because I haven't said anything I haven't noticed.' He took a deep breath. 'And about this morning, you and Val. . .'

'Yes?'

'I rather think that I overreacted. Sorry.'

He didn't want her to leave the practice, and was

actually apologising for his way-out behaviour this morning. Fantastic! Well, he mightn't like her much, but at least he now admitted to valuing her professionally. That was a step forward.

Miranda looked boldly into his stern, handsome face beneath the widow's peak of wiry black hair, seeing—as if for the first time—the well-marked arched eyebrows and the uncompromising mouth set in a firm line. Miracle of miracles, he was apologising and making it plain that he didn't want her to leave Combe Minster.

All at once, without really knowing why, she felt her usual strong, confident self. She smiled and said gently, 'Yes, I rather think you did overreact, though I can see that it was out of concern for Val and what you see as his vulnerability. You were just being a good friend.'

He growled, 'It doesn't excuse my boorish behaviour.'

'No, but it explains it.' It was extraordinary that this sophisticated, self-possessed man seemed to need reassuring. She laid a hand on his arm and said quietly, 'Look, Tom, why not leave Val to me? I've got his measure, and he's got mine. I promise I won't let him get hurt; he knows where he stands with me.'

Again smothering a longing to take her in his arms and kiss her breathless, Tom covered her slender hand with his and squeezed it hard. 'You're a remarkable woman, Miranda,' he said. 'I've just begun to realise how remarkable.'

His eyes smiled into hers and suddenly, effortlessly, they were in complete accord. There was an undercurrent of mutual understanding—colleagues sealing a pact of friendship—all differences, for the moment at least, forgotten.

The beeper on his watch pinged urgently. He stood up. 'Sorry, I didn't realise the time. I'll have to dash—

a couple of private insurance examinations to do. May I get you another drink before I go?'

Miranda stood up too. 'No, thanks, I'll be off now. There's a programme I want to watch on Channel Four.'

'Let me guess—the rerun of Kenneth Clark's *Civilisation.*'

'The same.'

'I've set my video to record it—great stuff.'

'So I believe. I was too young to appreciate it first time around.'

'Ouch!' He grimaced. 'That dates me. I was a very studious youngster hovering between architecture and medicine.'

She laughed. 'You don't look a day over—'

'Don't say it,' he groaned. 'I've reached the big four-oh.'

'I was going to say thirty-five,' she said with a laugh.

They parted outside The Cellary door in the chilly purple dusk, he to return to the surgery and she to the safe haven of her charming little cottage tucked away behind the cathedral.

As the next few weeks passed, and a red and gold September melted into a coppery October, Miranda found her days both on duty and off busy and happy.

Her working week quickly settled into a routine of nursing and administrative duties. Mondays were set aside for dealing with invoices and staff time and pay sheets, with help from the visiting bookkeeper.

Tuesdays and Wednesdays were divided between nursing in the general clinics, seeing pharmaceutical sales reps and placing orders for supplies and equipment. On Thursday afternoons she was knee-deep in small children in the busy mother and toddler clinic, and Fridays were spent tying up loose ends.

She had a regular meeting with Liz Fuller and Pat Payne in the morning, and a senior staff meeting with the doctors in the evening. All in all, it was a busy and satisfying timetable.

But Thursdays and the mother and toddler clinic was the high spot of her week. She found it intensely satisfying to work with the children and with Tom Brodie, who, she discovered, was an absolute wizard with the children.

He was casually cheerful, teasing, understanding of their fears but firm, and they trusted him. It was a pleasure to watch his capable, long-fingered hands examine their small bodies, and see them respond to the skilful, straightforward questions that he put to them in language that they could understand.

And yet he never talked down to them. Just as she had enjoyed working on the paediatric ward as a student nurse, she was now happy to have the chance of working with children again.

Not that these youngsters were as sick as those she had nursed in hospital. Many of them were fit and healthy and had simply come to be weighed and measured, given a medical check-up and receive inoculations and injections. Often it was the mothers who wanted reassurance or general advice on how to cope with the problems of small children—anything from teething to bed-wetting.

But there was an occasional exception to the rule when a really sick child would show up at the clinic. On the second Thursday in October a young woman, carrying a small baby in a grubby sling hanging from her shoulders, appeared just as Miranda was seeing off her last mother and three-year-old. Little more than a girl, she hovered in the doorway, pushing at the long, lank brown hair that half covered her face.

'Am I too late?' she asked uncertainly.

'Not at all,' replied Miranda with a reassuring smile. She peeped at the infant huddled against the girl's flat chest. A pair of large blue eyes stared solemnly up at her from a tiny, sallow, almost yellow little face. 'But you've come to the wrong clinic, I'm afraid. This is for toddlers, not babies. The babies are seen on Tuesdays or in general surgery times.'

'But Alice must see a doctor, she must. She had an operation soon after she was born and should have had a check-up but we moved on, and it's started again. . . her tummy. . .' She took the baby out of the sling, laid her on the table in front of Miranda and peeled back a shawl and shabby dress. 'Look!'

Miranda stared at the baby's swollen, grossly distorted abdomen. A long horizontal scar sliced across the tiny body from side to side. She touched the rigid, drum-like abdomen gently, guessing that it was full of fluid. 'How old is Alice, Mrs. . .?'

'Sandra Jeffries—I'm not married—we live with my boyfriend—she's five months—oh, please, please do something,' the girl begged, her voice shrill and staccato and her eyes, as big and blue as her baby's, full of fear. 'Don't let her die. I should have brought her sooner, only Kev said. . .'

'All right, Sandra, calm down, love. You've brought her, that's the main thing. I'll get Dr Brodie to look at her. He's an expert on children and he'll know exactly what to do. Now, you sit down and give Alice a cuddle while I go and have a word with him.'

Tom was writing up his notes in the little examination cubicle at the end of the long room. For the merest fraction of a second Miranda paused in the doorway, watching him. What a nice masculine head he's got, she thought; what a nice man he is.

He looked up expectantly with raised eyebrows and gave her a quirky smile. 'Late arrival?'

'Yes, I'm sorry. She's not really one of ours—a baby five months old—but I think you should see her. She's pretty poorly—jaundiced, ascites of abdomen, had surgery soon after birth, extensive laparotomy scar. The mum's in a bad way too. She's only a girl—about seventeen, by the look of her. From what she said, I think she's a New Age traveller. Oh, Tom, she's scared stiff, poor kid. She lives with a boyfriend who doesn't sound very supportive. Will you see what you can do, please?'

For a moment Tom stared at her in silence. Her sea-green eyes were misty with compassion, her voice soft and pleading. She was all woman and then some, he thought, and a great rush of love for this tender-hearted Miranda overwhelmed him. He said gruffly, 'Of course I'll see them. Wheel them in.'

With infinite care and gentleness he examined the baby, Alice, and with equal gentleness questioned Sandra. 'Did they explain to you at the hospital why they had operated on Alice?' he asked.

'They said she had something called biliary atresia, and her gall bladder wasn't working properly—or her liver—and the operation might put it right. And they said to take her back for a check-up and they gave me prescriptions for vitamins and antibiotics to put in with a special feed mixture, which they said would help, but I've run out and her tummy's swelling up again and she's gone yellow like she did before.'

The young girl looked from Tom to Miranda with frightened eyes. Her voice rose hysterically. 'Will she have to go into hospital again?'

Tom said with infinite gentleness, 'Yes, Sandra, I'm afraid she will. She's a very sick baby and she'll have to go in straight away. I'll phone the local hospital and arrange for her to be admitted immediately. How are you fixed for transport?'

'Kev's outside with the van.'

'And he *will* take you, Sandra, won't he? Your baby must go in at once. If there's any doubt about it I'll order an ambulance.'

'Oh, don't worry, Doctor, he will. He's scared like I am now he can see Alice is really ill.'

'Right, well, I'll make that phone call. Sister will tell you how to get to the hospital—it's across the other side of the town. Report to the accident and emergency department; they'll be expecting you.' Tom moved from the examination couch to the desk and picked up the telephone. He gave the frightened young mother a lovely reassuring smile. 'Take care, Sandra, and take heart. Alice will be in good hands, and a lot can be done now for a baby with her condition.'

'Thank you, Doctor. You and Nurse have been ever so kind,' said Sandra as she left the cubicle.

'How do you think she'll do—baby Alice?' asked Miranda, her voice soft with concern as she and Tom sat drinking tea in the cubicle-cum-office a little while later. It was incredibly peaceful without the clatter and chatter of many small children, and she wrapped her hands round her mug and sipped gratefully at her tea.

She gazed down into the straw-coloured liquid, savouring the moment, the peace, the quiet, Tom's presence and the gradually changing nature of her working relationship with him that had improved over the weeks since her meeting with him in The Cellary.

There was no doubt that she had won his professional trust completely. These days he even seemed to like her a little, which was immensely pleasing and warming. It was good to be liked by this man who had, at one time, seemed to have such an adversion to her. Maybe, if it hadn't been for Liz Fuller he would perhaps have more than liked her. . .

Ruthlessly she squashed the thought.

Tom looked at her bent head with loving eyes. He longed to stroke her shining honey-gold hair, cup her face with his hands and kiss her beautiful mouth, drooping a little now with tiredness after a busy afternoon. He cherished this interlude of quiet that they shared each week after the clinic. He felt closer to her then than at any other time as they reviewed their afternoon's work.

It was magic for him, but did it mean anything to her? he wondered. She was fantastic with the children—gentle, firm, loving—but with him she was always so cool, so detached—the complete career woman.

Abruptly he switched his mind back to her question about baby Alice. How would that poor little scrap do? He shrugged.

'Can't say. She'll probably have to have a liver transplant later on—most biliary atresia babies do—but the success rate there is good. Trouble is, this infant's background seems to be against her. Both she and her mother look undernourished to me, and if they're moving around. . .' He shrugged again and pulled a sad face. 'We can but hope.'

Miranda raised her head and smiled at him across the narrow desk, a smile of such sweetness that it took his breath away. 'And pray,' she said softly. 'One can always pray.'

'How true,' he agreed. 'Prayer's a pretty powerful aid to medicine—we don't use it enough.'

'Oh, I'm so surprised, but so glad, that you feel like that,' said Miranda, obviously delighted, her eyes shining.

'Why surprised?' asked Tom, relishing the idea that he had pleased her.

'I thought you might be too cynical, too disillusioned

to have faith in prayer. So many medical people are.'

Tom said thoughtfully, 'That's true. Yet we shouldn't be, not in our profession. Oh, we see enough of the downside of life, but we also see many unexplained miracles or near-miracles. Cures that shouldn't happen, but do. We meet extraordinary people who rise above all sorts of disabilities and disasters—who never give up. I saw plenty of that when I was with the WHO with doctors and nurses and other carers, as well as patients.'

His voice dropped. 'Oh, yes, I believe in the power of prayer—prayer and tender loving care and super technology in equal parts.'

As he finished speaking their eyes met and locked and merged, drawing them together over the narrow desk. There was a moment's hushed silence in the small cubicle. Miranda held her breath. *Déjà vu*, she thought; this has happened before.

In slow motion he raised his hand and lightly touched the peachy softness of her cheek. Her skin tingled where he'd touched it. 'Oh, Miranda,' he murmured huskily, 'I wish. . .' What the hell could he say? 'I wish I could tell you that I love you?' No, of course not.

Abruptly he dropped his hand. The moment was over. For the umpteenth time he'd nearly made a fool of himself. God, what must she think of him, his cool, remote, lovely Miranda? Say something practical, man, he told himself.

He pulled a face and, turning his mouth down and raising one expressive eyebrow, said passionately, 'I wish to God we could do more to help our patients. One sometimes feels so bloody useless.' He ran his fingers through his thick black hair and grated, 'How pathetic. Lord, I must be getting maudlin in my old age.'

Miranda expelled her inheld breath slowly and

dredged up a faint smile. 'No, not maudlin,' she said quietly, 'just caring.' She looked at her fob watch and stood up. 'I must go and tidy up outside and get back to my office. I've some never-ending paperwork to do before I beetle off home.'

Tom shrugged his impressive shoulders and gathered up the patients' notes that were piled on the desk. 'As you say, paperwork—that never-ending chore, the bane of every administrator's life.'

He stood up and gave her a wry smile. 'And I'd better be off to do mine before evening surgery.' He waved the bundle of notes at her. 'I'll drop these into Reception for filing on the way and leave you to your tidying up. Goodnight, Miranda.' And, giving her a brisk nod, he strode round the desk and out of the room.

Methodically and deliberately making her mind a blank, she tidied up the play area and packed away the weighing machine, measuring charts, record cards and other paraphernalia used in the clinic, then made her way back to her office.

There she sat for a long time, deep in thought, staring down at her paper-strewn desk. What *had* that brief interlude meant when she and Tom had gazed wordlessly into each other's eyes? That extraordinary feeling she'd had that time was standing still. Had he felt it too? His eyes, dark, dark brown and luminous, had seemed to devour her, caress her. And the way he had uttered her name—falteringly, unsteadily. For one mini-sec she had imagined. . .

His voice had been so husky and he had touched her cheek so gently, as if she was something precious. . . as if he wanted to. . .

No, she was mistaken, imagining things; she'd misread him. His gentleness had been triggered by compassion for his last tiny patient, little Alice Jeffries.

It had not been directed towards her personally; she had just happened to be there.

Her thoughts whizzed round like a Catherine wheel, and she could make no sense of them. What was happening to her? Why did this man effect her so strongly? You know why, jeered an infuriatingly calm little voice inside her, you're. . .'No, I'm not,' she muttered savagely. 'I'm not in love with Tom Brodie,' she ground out through gritted teeth.

She gripped the edge of her desk and said loudly and firmly, 'Of course you're not. Don't even think about it, woman. You're not in love with him. You like him a lot, nothing more. He fascinates you because he didn't grovel at your feet when you first met, and still doesn't. And if he loves anybody it's Liz Fuller; get that into your thick head, Miranda Gibbs.'

For a long time she continued to stare at the blur of papers on her desk as she tried to come to terms with her muddled thoughts. Thoughts that she had successfully buried until now. Thoughts and feelings about Tom that she had refused to acknowledge, but which had suddenly surfaced and which she must now face.

For, in spite of telling herself that she only wanted friendship from him, she knew that she was hovering on the brink of falling in love and had never felt so vulnerable. She, the dedicated career woman, was in danger of falling in love with a man who might appreciate her professionally, but found her only mildly interesting as a woman.

What the hell was she going to do about it?

Pushing this disturbing thought into the back of her mind, she concentrated on her paperwork and by six o'clock was able to pack up and thankfully take herself off duty and home to her cottage.

CHAPTER SIX

AN HOUR later Miranda, showered and scented and wearing stylish black velvet stirrup pants and a ruby-red silk shirt—topped by a multicoloured jacket—was on her way to the leisure centre, where she was to meet Val Thorpe and other friends.

She had joined the social club at the leisure centre soon after her arrival in Combe Minster, and Sue and Andrew Palmer had introduced her to their wide circle of acquaintances.

The male members of the club gave her a predictably warm welcome, the women a more guarded one. But their antipathy didn't last long. They soon discovered that she wasn't going to use her startling beauty to lure their partners away, and readily accepted her into their set.

In no time at all she began to make her own circle of friends, and was bombarded with invitations to wine and dine or meet up for coffee. And when she wasn't receiving hospitality she was returning it, by giving cosy little get-togethers in her cottage, so that her social life was soon as full as her working life.

Tom Brodie, Liz Fuller and Val Thorpe were leisure centre regulars and members of the Palmers' set, a sort of club within a club. But she had seen little of Tom or Liz since becoming a member. As talented tennis players representing the centre at county level in the mixed doubles on the indoor circuit, they were heavily engaged in an important series of matches.

Occasionally they appeared for a drink in the bar, but this was a rare happening as they were too busy practising or playing to socialise much.

She saw Val often, clubbing, partying and at his local, The Minster Arms, to which he'd introduced her and which she'd adopted as her local too. They had established a nice, easy, friendly relationship which worked well, though she was always conscious of the fact that he would be happy to make it more intimate if she gave so much as a hint. But she sidestepped this by avoiding tête-a-tête meetings with him, seeing him always in the company of mutual friends.

But although it was Val she was meeting at the club it was Tom who filled her thoughts as she made her way along the narrow cobbled streets around the cathedral.

Her mind chased back and forth over what had happened in the surgery that afternoon when they'd attended sick little baby Alice and her distraught young mother. So little had been said; so much suggested; so much held back. In the unlikely event that she met Tom this evening, would she be able to hide her feelings that had surfaced so alarmingly?

Yes, she would, she assured herself crossly. Only she was aware of the fact that she in love with him. All she needed to do was to continue in her role of reserved, dedicated nurse manager and no one need be any the wiser, least of all Tom himself.

She would stick to being a coolly friendly colleague, as she had since joining the practice. She would ignore the events of the afternoon and the vibes that had sizzled between them. Kill the possibility that he might have read anything special into their momentary eye contact.

Could she do it when she next came face to face with him—conceal the fact that she was in love with him? She had to; he wasn't a free agent—he was committed to Liz. Anyway, perhaps it wasn't love—not the real thing—but disturbed hormones playing games with her emotions. There was a thought!

After all, what was love—romantic love? It wasn't something tangible. You couldn't get hold of it, touch it, feel it—it was an emotion, an emotion that had eluded her till now, this intangible thing called love.

Anything was possible where love was concerned. You could fall into it or out of it at the drop of a hat.

Out of the blue, hope surged through her. Perhaps Tom and Liz would fall out of love. Then he *would* be a free agent.

She clamped down on this fanciful thought, but a little bubble of optimism remained with her as she walked briskly along the medieval street. She suddenly felt elated. All was going to be well; she could feel it in her bones.

There was a sliver of a new moon hanging in the star-studded indigo sky over the jagged rooftops, competing with the amber glow from the streetlights. A new moon—wasn't that supposed to bring good luck? The night air was scented with bonfire smoke which drifted over garden walls. It was a beautiful night, a night full of promise.

She marvelled, as she always did, how so much was packed into a small radius around the cathedral—the major shops, leisure centre, theatre—all within walking distance of her cottage. It was cosy and intimate and she loved it. It was so unlike the huge sprawl of Birmingham which she'd left behind only weeks before. She already felt that she belonged to Combe Minster and the cathedral practice and the friends she had made at the club.

This was now her world and she was going to enjoy it—not let anything upset her satisfying, peaceful, hard-won independence, she vowed silently as she neared the centre. Somehow she would come to terms with her feelings for Tom Brodie; make the most of working with him and enjoying his company socially when and if they were thrown together, but strictly as a friend. Anything would be better than leaving this safe haven and not seeing him at all.

Ironically, she clapped eyes on him directly she arrived at the leisure centre.

He was sitting alone at the bar in the club room where she had arranged to meet Val, gazing down into a mug of beer that he was cradling in his hands.

The unexpected sight of him, coming hot on the heels of her see-sawing thoughts, shocked her into a breathless silence. Heart in mouth, she stood stock-still in the doorway and stared, mesmerised, at the back of his handsome head, very black and sleek against the white of his sweater. She found herself willing him to look up and see her.

And a moment later he did look up, straight into the lighted mirror above the bar and straight at her reflection there among the multicoloured bottles. Slowly he put down his glass and, turning his head, smiled at her across the half-empty room—a wide, welcoming smile of pure pleasure that lit up his lean, austere face.

Her heart lurched. A tide of joy flooded through her. She smiled back at him, lips parted in a warm, gentle, tremulous smile. She forgot her intention of playing it cool as, still smiling, she walked slowly toward him.

Tom slid from the stool and watched her as she approached with long graceful strides. His pulse raced, missed a beat or two. God, she was beautiful, and she was smiling at him. Could it be *for* him? He couldn't help himself, but held out both his hands to her and said huskily, 'Miranda.'

'Tom. . .' It was a whisper. Without thinking, she slipped her hands into his.

He grasped them firmly, looked down at her,

caressed her with his look and rubbed his thumbs back and forth across her knuckles.

He repeated, with a kind of wonder in his voice and his eyes never leaving her face, 'Miranda.'

Breathlessly she stared up into his face and drowned in his eyes, sensing his wonder and feeling it herself—marvelling at it.

'Yes?' Her voice trembled.

'Can I get you drink?'

The prosaic words seemed to be forced out of him. She knew that was not what he wanted to say.

Her eyes dropped down to his mouth, the mouth that had uttered those mundane words—and lingered there. She longed to kiss those firm lips. . . Don't even dream of it, she warned herself. She let out a long, slow breath. 'Please. . .a very dry vermouth.' She made her voice flat, steady.

'Ice and lemon, as before?' So, he'd remembered her order in the wine bar weeks ago.

'As before.'

Slowly he let her hands slip out of his and gently pressed her onto the stool beside him. She was glad to sit down; her legs felt shaky. She watched him covertly out of the corner of her eye as he ordered her drink. In profile he looked as he usually did, immensely calm, firm-lipped, firm-chinned and strong.

Had he really spoken her name so tenderly; caressed her with his eyes; taken her hands in his? Doubt washed over her. Well, he'd held her hands—she hadn't imagined that. But did it mean anything, or was it a simply friendly gesture? Had she exaggerated the tender voice, the smouldering eyes?

Was she simply seeing what she wanted to see? Had it all been in her mind?

She took a long, deep breath to steady herself and

turned a serene face towards him when he handed her her drink a moment later.

He gave her a lopsided, thoughtful sort of smile. 'It suits you,' he said softly.

'What?' With pretended calm, she gave him a sidelong glance over the rim of her glass as she took a sip of the colourless liquid.

'Dry vermouth—ice-cold, sharp with lemon, sophisticated—just right for a dedicated career lady with beautiful sea-green eyes.'

Was he gently teasing or cruelly taunting? She looked hard into the depths of his velvet brown eyes, but could read absolutely nothing there. He didn't seem to be the same man who only minutes before had held her hands and had huskily, lovingly, uttered her name. She *had* been kidding herself.

Shattered, she whispered, 'Is that how you see me—as sharp and ice-cold?' She put down her drink and swivelled round to face him square-on.

He turned too, leaned forward and lightly touched a curling tendril of hair that lay against her cheek—pinching it between his forefinger and thumb, pulling it straight then letting it spring back into place.

She refused to tremble or draw away at his touch.

'Not always,' he murmured. 'The ice cracks occasionally, revealing the real woman. When you're working with patients, for instance, you're incredibly gentle—especially with the children. And, of course, you have a natural charisma, tons of it, which is what draws people to you—women as well as men.'

He continued thoughtfully, 'They see past the beautiful exterior to the warm inner you. That's what I didn't see when I first met you—your soft centre. I thought you would use your beauty—that it would be a threat to the vulnerable and to the practice—but it's only a threat to you, Miranda, isn't it?'

No longer enigmatic, his eyes were full of compassion.

Miranda stared at him. Was he really so perceptive? Did he really understand what a fight it had been to convince her peers of her true worth in spite of her beauty? Did he appreciate the jealousy it had sometimes aroused, or the conviction some arrogant men held that she was brainless because she was beautiful?

It would be wonderful if he did.

'Do you really think—?' she started to say when, over his shoulder, she saw a familiar figure standing in the doorway. A sudden pang of disappointment, laced with anger, swept over her.

She might have known it—where Tom Brodie was, Liz Fuller wouldn't be far away. Had she been there long; had she seen Tom touching her hair? Perhaps not. The club room was now pretty crowded. Miranda took a deep breath and said quietly, 'Liz is here, Tom. I presume she's looking for you.'

'Yes, we're meeting for a drink.' His voice was flat, expressionless. He turned on the stool, stood up and waved to Liz.

He doesn't sound very lover-like, thought Miranda wryly, not wildly delighted to see her—or is that too just wishful thinking on my part?

'We must continue this conversation some other time,' he murmured as they watched Liz making her way toward them.

Miranda came down to earth with a bang. No, she thought fiercely, that's just what we mustn't do. No more intimacies. Don't get any ideas about this man, whatever you read into what he said or did and however understanding he seems to be; don't let him get under your skin; forget it. You'll only get hurt.

Tom Brodie is his own man or, if he's anybody's, he's Liz Fuller's. Whatever passed between you and him was chemistry, nothing more. It's nothing but physical attraction on his part, and you know all about men and that. He and Liz have a thing going between them. Accept that fact for your own peace of mind and for the good of the practice. You don't want to, can't afford to rock the boat.

Remember that you're the responsible, dedicated nurse manager, with everything to lose and nothing to gain by allowing yourself to be sidetracked by your emotions. Be tough with yourself, starting right now.

She pinned a welcoming smile on her face as Liz reached the bar. 'Hello, Liz,' she said brightly. 'I'm waiting for Val, and Tom has been keeping me company.'

Liz said, 'Oh, really,' sounding faintly amused, or was it suspicious? She tossed her head, shaking her abundant mane of black hair. Her long dangling earrings jangled and her eyes glittered. 'Good, I hope he's been keeping you entertained.' She lifted a smiling face to Tom, clearly inviting a kiss. 'Hi,' she murmured huskily, 'sorry I'm late.'

Tom bent his head and just touched her cheek with his lips. 'Oh, but you're not, I was early,' he said. 'Now, what'll you have to drink?'

Liz widened her eyes in surprise. 'Tom, you know that you don't have to ask. I'll have my usual, of course.'

She's signalling her claim on him, thought Miranda, warning me off.

He was ordering a Clementine when Val, Sue and Andrew Palmer and Josie and Elmer Floyd arrived. Miranda was enormously relieved and pleased to see them. Their appearance made it easier to be bright and cheerful and carefree as they sipped their drinks and chatted in the easy manner of old friends. But she remained skin-tinglingly aware of Tom's presence and his occasional deep throaty laugh.

'Come and eat with us,' Val suggested, on learning that Tom and Liz weren't playing tennis as usual. 'We've booked a table at the new Indian place in the high street. I'm sure they'll manage another two places.'

Tom was pleased with the suggestion. 'Great idea, I'd like that. What about you, Liz?'

Liz shrugged. 'I suppose we could give it a whirl.' She sounded reluctant.

She wants him to herself and I don't blame her, thought Miranda, feeling an odd shaft of sympathy for her colleague.

Tom seemed not to notice Liz's reluctance. 'Good, we'd love to join you,' he said. 'It'll make a nice change to have a normal evening out. We haven't had the chance recently. Too much tennis. In fact, I'll be heartily glad when this marathon comes to an end.' He removed his spectacles and glanced smilingly round at everyone, and his amused brown eyes met Miranda's for an instant.

Her fingers tightened round the stem of her glass, but she smiled composedly back at him.

'So, *why* aren't you two playing tonight?' Elmer asked, looking from Tom to Liz.

'I'm suffering from a bit of muscle strain in my right arm and Tom won't let me play,' replied Liz with a shrug. 'It's nothing much, but he's so protective of me.' She gave Tom a dimpled smile and laid a hand on his arm.

'Can't afford to take any chances so near the finals,' he said evenly. 'And a couple of days off won't hurt us.'

'Well, you don't want to risk getting tennis elbow,' said Josie. 'That would put you out of action for weeks. We had a friend who had it, though it wasn't caused through tennis but, of all things, by playing darts. His doctor called it epi. . .something, though it's commonly known as tennis elbow.'

'Epicondylitis,' said Tom and Val in unison.

'And what's that exactly?' asked Elmer. 'Come on, one of you clever medics fill us ignorant laymen in on the background.'

Tom raised an enquiring eyebrow. 'Are you sure? Won't it bore you stiff?'

'Not a bit,' said Sue firmly. 'All things medical are fascinating to the non-professionals—that's why there are so many medical programmes on television, like *Casualty* and so on.'

Tom shrugged. 'Well, if you're sure. . .OK, epicondylitis is inflammation of the elbow joint and surrounding tissues, caused by constant use or misuse of the muscles which are attached to the humerus by the tendons, which get strained. Mostly happens in racquet sports, hence the term "tennis elbow", though it can occur in other sports and even some professions where the arms are used excessively.'

He glanced round. Surely they'd had enough.

'Such as?' said Elmer.

'Well, I had a patient once, a professional violinist, who had a really severe case. His bow arm suddenly seized up and was excruciatingly painful. He didn't respond to rest, analgesics, ice packs, ultraviolet or corticosteroids, and in the end the poor chap had to have surgery.'

'By surgery, you mean an operation,' said Sue.

Tom nodded. 'Yes, a procedure called tendolysis. It's performed to free a tendon from the adhesions which are limiting movement and causing pain. A tricky little op that involves stripping away the fibrous sheath that's adhered to the tendon, causing the tenosynovitis. It's usually successful, but there's no guarantee that the adhesions won't return again.'

'So, what happened to your violinist?'

'He's moved away so I don't know what the long-term prognosis is, but he was beginning to play again before he left.'

'So the operation was successful?' said Sue.

'In the short term, certainly,' said Tom, 'but—'

Andrew, whippet thin but who ate like the proverbial horse, interrupted at that point, draining his glass and saying in a dry, drawling voice, 'Look, I don't want to be rude. All this medical stuff is enthralling, but can't we continue with this discussion at the restaurant? I'm absolutely starving. Let's go and eat.'

The restaurant was warm, dim and aromatic with delicious spicy smells drifting in from the kitchen. Little red shaded glass globe lamps glowed like jewels on each table. There were several lamps on the long table that had been laid for six, and plenty of room for the two extra people.

Miranda found herself sitting between Val and Elmer and directly opposite Tom and Liz. Well, at least I'm not sitting beside him, she thought with relief. God knows how I would have coped with that. Yet, strangely, her relief was tinged with disappointment, and for a fleeting moment she imagined the joy of being close to him, touching him. . . She pulled her thoughts up with a jerk, and answered some trivial comment of Val's.

But sitting opposite Tom brought its own intimacies, she realised with a surge of excitement, for whenever she looked up his eyes seemed to be upon her. His dark brown, almost black eyes reflected in miniature the rose red of the lamp that stood between them, twinkling tiny images that seemed to wink at her from their dark depths.

She was inordinately pleased that she had dressed

with care. She knew that she looked good in the simple red silk shirt that shimmered in the lamplight, enhancing the creamy bronzed perfection of her complexion and the shiny honey-gold of her hair.

Conversation was animated and the atmosphere took on a festive air as their drinks appeared—tall glasses of ice-cold Indian beer—and smiling waiters deftly laid the table with fragrant food.

Dish after dish appeared and was placed hot and steaming on the candlelit warming trays. Chicken tikka, biriani, crisp samosas, bhujia with bright green peas and rich red tomatoes, minced meat kebabs and platters of fried and boiled rice. There were baskets of poppadoms, nan bread, an array of dips and sauces and a magnificent banana pudding for dessert.

It was a happy occasion, a coming together of good friends and good food.

Even Liz, who had been quiet and sulky earlier, grew vivacious and ebullient as the evening progressed. She positively blossomed under the attention she was receiving from Andrew Palmer who, when he chose, could in his dry way be utterly charming and a consummate flirt. An innocent act which deceived no one, least of all his wife whom everyone knew he adored.

She's trying to make Tom jealous, thought Miranda, watching Liz out of the corner of her eye and, in all fairness, why not? He's not exactly been behaving like a man in love this evening: he hasn't touched Liz once since he kissed her when she first arrived, and that wasn't much of a kiss. But perhaps that's because there are other people around. When they're alone I bet he's loving and warm and passionate. . .

Val whispered in her ear, 'Penny for them, Miranda.'

She jumped and improvised, 'I was just thinking how stunning Liz looks tonight, and how amusing Andrew can be when he tries.'

Val looked thoughtful. He glanced across the table. 'And how hard Liz's working to attract Tom's attention,' he said drily. 'Not that it'll do her any good, poor girl. What little chance she ever had has gone. But you've got to give her an A for effort; she never gives up.'

Miranda looked at him with surprised eyes. 'I don't know what you mean. They have an understanding, haven't they? Liz said. . .'

'Wishful thinking on Liz's part. She's fancied Tom ever since she joined us in our old practice a couple of years ago. When they started partnering each other for tennis it threw them together, and everyone began treating them as an item. Tom went along with it but I'm damned sure that he hasn't made any sort of commitment, nor ever will.'

Miranda's heart was beating very fast. . . If Tom wasn't in love with Liz, then maybe. . .

She steadied her voice and asked, 'What makes you so sure about that?'

Val shrugged dismissively. 'I know the man. He's my friend. He's had a few discreet affairs over the years, but he's a confirmed bachelor and dedicated doctor. Of course that might change but, as far as I know, he's just not interested in a long-term relationship, unlike me. I couldn't wait to find someone, get married and settle down. . .' He broke off, his usually happy face serious, sad.

'I'm so sorry, Val.' Miranda laid a hand on his arm. 'You'll meet somebody one day.'

He covered her hand with his. 'I already have,' he murmured, looking her straight in the eye, 'but she's not interested.'

'Oh, Val, no,' she said in a low, anguished voice, sliding her hand out from beneath his. 'I never meant this to happen.'

He produced a rueful smile. 'It's OK, not your fault.

You were straight right from the start, love. Just as long as we remain friends, whatever happens.'

'Always,' promised Miranda. 'I mean that, Val.'

Though her head was turned toward Val, she was acutely aware that Tom was watching her from the other side of the table and the skin prickled at the back of her neck. What was he making of her obviously intimate conversation with Val—their touching hands? She hoped he didn't think. . . She felt herself blush and picked up her tall, slender glass of beer, rolling it against her hot cheeks.

Val picked up his glass and clinked it against hers. He said softly, 'That's all I ask. Here's to friendship.'

'To friendship,' said Miranda, and took a sip of the cool golden liquid.

The rest of the evening passed in a haze as she let the conversation drift and eddy about her. With half her mind she concentrated on what was being said and made polite noises, and with the other half she pondered on the startling information that Val had imparted about Liz and Tom.

So much was explained if it was true that there wasn't an understanding between them and that they weren't practically engaged, as Liz had implied. No wonder he was so casual toward her; no wonder she was so fiercely possessive of him.

He's a free agent, she realised, her heart beating fast in her breast. No wonder he feels free to flirt with me. *No*, not flirt, that's wrong. He wasn't flirting when we met this evening. He was tender, gentle. . .almost lover-like. We both felt it and it wasn't flirting. It was something inevitable; it had a dreamlike quality but it was real; if Liz hadn't appeared. . .

The party broke up just before eleven o'clock.

Grouped on the narrow pavement, they said their

prolonged goodbyes outside the restaurant. Everyone was talking at once. For an instant Tom stood beside Miranda, and his hand just brushed against hers. Tiny, hairlike fingers of electricity flickered up her arm.

She tensed, quivered.

'Cold?' he murmured.

She shook her head and moved fractionally away from him. In the muted light of the streetlamps she saw his eyes gleam and his mouth curve into a slow smile.

Liz, who'd been in animated conversation with Andrew, moved back to Tom's side and slipped her arm through his. She smiled coyly up at him. 'Isn't it time we went, darling?' Her speech was a little slurred. She peered round him at Miranda. 'Tom insists on taking me home,' she explained loudly, an edge of triumph in her voice, 'as my car's on the blink. I came in by taxi and I could go home the same way, but he won't hear of it.'

Miranda felt embarrassed for her and for Tom—she was so clearly making up to him. 'Oh, good,' she said lamely.

Sue Palmer said drily, 'Tricky getting a taxi this time of night. Good job Tom can take you home. But how will you get in in the morning?'

'Oh, the mechanic at the local garage said he'd work on it this evening; he doesn't think there's much wrong.'

'Well, you *do* surprise me,' commented Sue sarcastically, and Miranda realised that she had bitterly resented Liz's monopoly of Andrew during dinner, and was hitting back at her.

At that point Elmer and Josie, who lived near the outskirts of the city north of the cathedral, said their final goodbyes and walked briskly away.

'We'll get going, too,' said Tom. 'It's been a splendid evening. Must do it again as soon as this damned tournament's over. It'll be good to get back into circulation and socialise normally.'

Liz was still hanging on his arm, but he extricated himself and put a supporting arm round her waist. Then, surprisingly gently, he said, 'Come on, Liz, time to get you home. Goodnight, everyone,' and, steering her along, they disappeared round the corner in the direction of the restaurant car park.

'She's drunk,' Sue said disgustedly.

'Don't see how she can be. She only drank about half a beer with supper,' said Andrew.

'Some people,' said Val thoughtfully, 'can't take alcohol at all—body chemistry and all that. Perhaps Liz is one of them. Anyway, Tom will see her home all right. And talking of home, I can offer you three a lift—my car's along at the surgery.'

Andrew turned down the offer. 'Thanks, Val, but I think Sue and I will walk. It's such a lovely night—real autumnal smell, that wood smoke.'

'And, if I may, I'll join you,' said Miranda, 'and walk off some of those calories.'

Val was disappointed, she could see, but he said wryly, 'So I've no takers. You fitness fanatics. OK, then, see you in the morning, Miranda. 'Night.' He lifted a hand in farewell, and strode away up the high street.

Sleep eluded Miranda. The cathedral clock chimed two. She got out of bed, padded to the open window and leaned out. The streetlights had gone off and the sky was full of stars, millions of them.

Her mind revolved round what Val had told her about Tom. Was he a lone, dedicated doctor bachelor who discreetly played the field but who had no interest in commitment? Had he been simply flirting with her this evening? No, she couldn't believe that. The way he had held her hands when they met in the club bar had been so tender, so sincere, and his eyes had spoken volumes. And though he had accused her of being cold and distant it was not in a critical manner, but as if he cared.

What was she to make of this detached, enigmatic man, with whom she had fallen so utterly in love? She had no previous experience of being in love, though many men—attracted by her singular beauty—had declared their love for her. *That* she could handle, but learning to deal with her own deep emotions was a different matter altogether.

However painful it is, you'll just have to continue to play it cool, she told herself. Play a waiting game. Hide your love; don't let Tom see how vulnerable you are to him. Wait for him to declare himself. He will if he is halfway in love with you, and if he isn't you'll just have to learn to live with it.

This resolve calmed her a little and stilled her chaotic thoughts to some extent. For a while she continued to gaze out of the window at the ghostly towers of the cathedral, glimmering against the night sky, and then, with a sigh, she returned to bed and slept fitfully till morning.

CHAPTER SEVEN

WEARING a warm track suit and trainers, Miranda left for work early the next morning, jogging in rubber-soled silence through the almost empty streets. It was grey and chilly and mist swirled round the pinnacles on the cathedral towers, making them look as if they were floating, ethereal and unreal.

She felt like the towers—detached from reality, she thought wryly, numb after a night of too much thinking of Tom Brodie, and Val's remarks, and too little sleep. But now she schooled her mind into a blessed blank and gave herself up to the soothing physical pleasure of running in steady rhythmical strides over the smooth cobbles.

The cathedral clock chimed seven as she reached the front door of the health centre. The building seemed deserted. She breathed a sigh of relief. Good, she would have time to begin stocktaking the drugs and dressings cupboards in peace before the rush started. It was chore that was always difficult to fit in, a chore that would keep her busy and mentally alert with no time to think personal disturbing thoughts.

She fished out the key from her body-belt, unlocked the double doors to the vestibule and walked through to the waiting-room.

But the waiting-room wasn't empty, as she had expected.

Tom was there, leaning against the reception desk and holding the telephone receiver to his ear, frowning and writing something in the visiting book.

Miranda stood quite still, staring at him as she had

last night at the club and, as then, her heart seemed to turn over, stop for a moment then beat a rapid tattoo against her ribs. So much for blanking him out of her mind. She hadn't expected to find anyone in the building, least of all Tom. He was covering the emergency surgery this morning, and not due to start till nine-thirty.

Still frowning as he listened to the voice at the other end of the line, he looked up and focused on Miranda who stood like a statue in the doorway.

He wasn't surprised to see her for, dreaming and waking, she'd been with him most of the night. Now she was here in the flesh, looking luscious, fresh and radiantly beautiful in a shocking-pink track suit—a slightly flushed golden goddess, with droplets of mist beading her hair like jewels.

An aching desire for her flooded over him. He wanted to shout a greeting of love, rush forward to meet her, sweep her into his arms, smother her with kisses. . .

Not possible, he reminded himself sharply, not here, not now. He was still unsure of her, in spite of the shared magical moments of last evening and their intense awareness of each other when they had talked together in the bar and later in the restaurant.

He allowed himself to smile faintly, and mouthed, 'Good morning.'

'Good morning,' she mouthed back, nodding and returning his smile. She squashed a longing to fly to him, throw herself into his arms and nestle against his broad chest. Heaven knows how he would react if I did, she thought wryly as she forced herself to walk sedately across the room, heading for the safety of her office and a chance to collect herself.

But Tom signalled her to wait as she made to pass him, laying a hand briefly on her arm.

Acutely aware of his touch and wondering why he

wanted her to wait, she muttered breathily, 'I must go and change.'

He shook his head, covered the mouthpiece of the receiver and in a low voice said firmly, 'No—wait.' He removed his hand from the phone and said to the caller, 'Right, Mrs Hodgson, someone will visit you later. Meanwhile, keep her in bed, give her an aspirin or paracetamol and plenty to drink. The more fluid you can get into her the better. Goodbye.'

Replacing the receiver, he stared thoughtfully at Miranda who stood so calm and detached beside him. What the hell was she thinking? Would he ever break through that cool reserve? Last night he'd thought. . .

He smothered his thoughts and said drily, 'Couldn't sleep so I decided to come in early and get on with some paperwork, but I haven't had a chance—that's the fourth call I've taken, asking for a visit. All reporting sky-high temperature, chestiness, sore throat, headache, shivering and, in some cases, vomiting—all the signs of a flu bug or some rogue virus going around. Let's hope it's flu. At least we know where we are with that, and can treat the symptoms.'

So he didn't want to speak to her about anything personal. They were on duty. Last night was over, forgotten; it was business as usual. She might have known.

She swallowed her disappointment. 'Let's hope,' she murmured. She raised crystal clear, sea-green eyes to his. 'Are we talking a local serious outbreak of something nasty?' she asked.

'Too soon to say. I've spoken to Kay on her mobile phone—that's when I switched the night calls through here to give her a break. She was with a patient—same symptoms—and she's had other calls during the night.'

His fine mouth turned down at the corners. 'Don't want to be an alarmist, but it doesn't look good; in a small community like this infection spreads so rapidly.

We'd better have a meeting when the others get in. Decide how to deal with the most vulnerable—children, chronic sick, elderly. Can you lay that on without disturbing the morning appointments list too disastrously?'

He was very much the doctor—the efficient, caring professional, the assistant head of practice.

Miranda nodded, the nurse in her appreciating his very real fear of a local outbreak of any infectious disease and the pressure it would put on the staff, especially the doctors. GPs were always in the front line of this sort of attack. The sooner they went into action the better. Best be prepared, even if the outbreak didn't amount to anything.

'We should ring around now and see if some of them can get in early, so that we can have the meeting before surgery gets properly under way. That would be least disruptive. If you contact Dr Withers, Bill and Lydia, I'll do the rest of the medical team and also alert Liz and Pat Payne. They can sort things out on the nursing and reception fronts between them and postpone a few non-urgent appointments where possible, leaving the doctors free to do visits.'

'Sounds sensible, but we mustn't alarm people unnecessarily.'

'Don't worry, it will all be low-key,' promised Miranda.

The phone shrilled into life.

Tom snatched it up. 'Combe Minster Medical Centre, Dr Brodie speaking.' He stared blankly into space, doodling on a notepad as he listened to a muffled voice at the other end of the line. At one point he said sharply, 'Yes, we have, about a dozen during the night.' And then added a few moments later, 'Well, thanks for letting me know; we'll keep you informed.'

He replaced the receiver and turned to face Miranda.

'That,' he said tersely, 'was an official from the county medical officer's department, confirming several flu outbreaks across the West Country and warning us to be prepared for an outbreak here. Apparently, it's been building up for several days but has only just reached serious proportions. They want a report every twenty-four hours on numbers, starting tonight. That'll be your pigeon, Miranda—another chore to add to your workload.'

'No problem,' she replied calmly. 'I'll cope, and at least we know now that it's flu and can start tackling it as such and not waste time looking for some elusive virus.'

Unexpectedly Tom chuckled, a low throaty chuckle. He took off his spectacles and laid them on the desk. His eyes, a moment before sombre and thoughtful, were soft and luminous—full of tenderness as he smiled down at her.

Her heart hammered, and for a long silent moment she stared up into his beloved face.

Then she found herself smiling back at him—slowly, tentatively, wonderingly. What was happening to her? She had meant to keep her distance from him, Val had said that he wasn't into long-term relationships—a confirmed bachelor. But she couldn't resist him; she was helpless. He just had to smile at her and her bones melted and her senses reeled.

He cupped her chin with infinitely gentle hands and brought his face close to hers. With great clarity she noticed the fine lines radiating from the corners of his eyes and round the strongly marked mouth. And she noticed, too, the few strands of silver glinting in the black hair that sprang so vigorously from his high forehead.

'Oh, Miranda,' he whispered, his warm breath rippling over her face. 'My lovely, beautiful, unflappable Miranda. What a treasure you are. . .'

He dropped his hands to her waist and drew her even closer, bending his head until his lips brushed hers in a feather-light butterfly kiss.

Miranda closed her eyes. 'We shouldn't,' she mumbled. 'Not here—work—lots to do. . .'

He kissed her eyelids, her forehead, her hairline, her nose. 'Such a pretty nose,' he murmured. He trailed his lips down to her mouth and traced its shape with the tip of his tongue, lingering at the corners.

The phone rang—once, twice, three times. . .

He lifted his head a little and fractionally loosened his hands from round her waist. 'Oh, hell,' he growled. 'Not now. Give us a break.'

Miranda exhaled a long deep breath and swallowed hard. 'Must answer,' she whispered. She eased herself very deliberately out of his arms, and raised a crooked little smile. 'After all, Dr Brodie, we are on duty.'

'So we are,' he agreed. In slow motion, his eyes still boring into hers, he stretched out a hand to pick up the receiver.

Miranda shook her head, forcing herself to break the union of their eyes. 'No,' she said, suddenly brisk and decisive, 'I'll deal with this. You phone Dr Withers and the others and put them in the picture. I'll field the calls here until the early receptionist arrives.'

He smiled slowly, his expressive eyes—still feasting on her face—glinting with humour and admiration. 'Ah,' he said drily, 'so the kissing has to stop! There speaks the voice of our efficient nurse manager. Must get our priorities right.'

He inclined his head in an ironic little bow. 'To hear is to obey, but I'll be back for more—much more.' Dropping a kiss on her cheek, he turned and strode from the room.

For a moment she gazed after him. She hated to see

him walk away from her and ached to call him back; longed to continue the kissing where it had left off seconds before. She gave herself a mental shake. Mustn't even think about it.

She lifted the receiver. 'Combe Minster Medical Centre.'

By eight-fifteen the meeting in the conference room at the top of the house was under way. All the doctors were there, even Stella Knight—the practice maternity specialist—who wasn't due in her maternity clinic at eleven. And Kay Brent, bleary-eyed after being on night calls, had given up her shower and change of clothes to be present.

Dr Withers, thought Miranda, eyeing the head of practice anxiously, didn't seem well. He looked old and grey and every bit his sixty-four years and more.

'You take over, Tom,' he said tiredly when they were all seated round the long table. 'Explain the situation and how you plan to tackle it. I'll go along with whatever you decide.'

Tom frowned. 'Are you all right, Dennis?' he asked. 'You don't look too good.'

Dr Withers scowled. 'Bad night, that's all. Get on with it, man; we've all got work to do.'

'OK,' said Tom mildly. He looked round the table, gathering everyone's attention. 'Well, you all have a good idea what the situation is. We've had a dozen or so patients presenting with flu symptoms in the last few hours, and have been warned by County Hall that an epidemic *might* be imminent. But don't assume that yet—just be on the alert.'

'Like continue to press the elderly and other vulnerables to have flu jabs,' suggested the junior partner, Leigh Stewart. 'Or is that a bit like bolting the door after the horse has fled?'

'No, not at all. The flu season hasn't really begun. This is an early outbreak—a fluke episode, perhaps. Mild cases should respond to bed-rest and analgesics. And, assuming that it's the A and B strain virus, sixty to seventy per cent of cases will react favourably to the current vaccine. Prophylactic containment is still our best bet, even if it's not effective immediately.'

Tom turned to Miranda and peered at her over the top of his heavy-rimmed glasses. It was an enquiring look, purely professional and giving nothing away but her heart did a momentary flip. 'How's the regular vaccination programme going, Miranda?' he asked. 'Is it well under way? Since you're in charge of the anti-flu jabs you must have the best idea of overall number of patients turning up for vaccination.'

'Well, the numbers have been rising since the beginning of October,' she replied, 'though we started giving jabs in September. A lot of people seem to have delayed coming in on account of the fine weather to date. And, as per routine, all patients have been reminded that vaccination is available. And we've recently put up posters in our country surgeries and local chemists.'

'And has there been a good response to that?'

'Yes, in this last week. Several nursing and retirement homes have been in touch, and batch prescriptions are in the pipeline for signature. We've plenty of vaccine in stock, and I've more on order. We could start visiting the residential homes and giving jabs immediately, instead of waiting till next week as planned.'

'Good, the sooner the better. Lay that on, please, even if it involves overtime pay—agreed?' He looked at his colleagues seated round the table. Everyone nodded. 'By the way, County Hall wants numbers of confirmed flu cases at the end of each day after afternoon visits or surgeries.'

There was a concerted groan. 'Not more bloody paperwork,' several muttered.

Miranda smiled round at them. 'Don't worry,' she spoke soothingly. 'Just let me have the numbers and I'll deal with the rest.'

'You're a gem,' said Val, his voice warm with praise. 'Don't know what we'd do without you.'

With the exception of Dr Withers, who sat with his elbows on the table supporting his bowed head, the other doctors indicated their agreement.

'I'll second that.' Bill Jones, gave her one of his slow, lazy smiles. 'She's a great gal.'

Dennis Withers muttered irritably, 'Oh, do get on.'

Tom said briskly, 'Yes, we must. I suggest we carry on as usual today; see what turns up and review matters this evening when we can decide if we've got a mild outbreak or an epidemic on our hands.'

Chris Elliot, the trainee G.P. on his first general practice assignment, asked tentatively, 'What's the drill if we get a chronic heart or lung patient with flu who is naturally prone to other infections?'

Tom said promptly, 'If you see the patient within twenty-four hours of symptoms developing, start them immediately on the antiviral drug, amantadine. If they produce a bacterial bug, don't hang about. Put them on an appropriate antibiotic, stat.'

He gave the young man, fresh out of the hectic but protected world of hospital where there was always a senior to refer to, a friendly smile. 'But if in doubt ask one of us for a second opinion, however busy we are. Never fear, you're not on your own.'

He glanced round the table. 'Anybody else have any suggestions or queries?' There was a general murmur and shaking of heads. 'Right, then it's business as usual. Meeting closed; let's get on with the day, and hope that things simmer down and this is something of a false alarm.'

But it wasn't.

The phone went constantly. All the morning, sandwiched between regular calls, there was an increasing trickle of requests for visits from patients reporting flu symptoms.

At eleven o'clock Pat Payne appeared in Miranda's office.

'We've got a problem,' she announced. 'The normal visiting lists for all the doctors doing calls today are chock-a-block—we can't fit anyone else in. What are we going to do—put people off till tomorrow, extend visits after evening surgeries?'

Miranda grimaced. 'I was afraid this might happen. I'll speak to Dr Withers. Meanwhile, tell patients with flu symptoms to stay in bed and drink plenty, and take a mild painkiller like aspirin or paracetamol if they have a headache or aching limbs. Explain that a doctor will visit as soon as possible.'

Pat said doubtfully, 'But you and the medics are dead against the reception staff giving out advice. Are you sure it's OK?'

'Positive. In this case, any of the doctors will endorse it. It's very general—the sort of advice any magazine or family encyclopedia might give.'

'All right, if you say so.'

They left the office together, Pat to Reception and Miranda—rather reluctantly—to Dr Withers's consulting-room. He hadn't seemed well this morning and had turned the meeting over to Tom, but he was head of practice and professional etiquette dictated that he should be put in the picture first.

'Come,' he called abruptly when she knocked at his door.

He was sitting at his desk, reading a letter, and didn't

look up when she entered. 'Yes,' he snapped, 'what is it?'

Miranda was appalled to see that the hand holding the letter was shaking, and his face looked cold and sweaty. He looked worse than he had earlier that morning when he'd refused to acknowledge that he wasn't well. He'd probably bite her head off, but the nurse in her wanted to do something practical.

She suggested gently, 'You look as if you could do with a cup of coffee, Dr Withers; shall I fetch you one?'

He glanced up at her and grated, 'No—no, thank you, Sister. Stop fussing and just tell me what it is you want.'

The silly, stubborn man. Well, she'd tried. Perhaps he wasn't as bad as he looked.

She said briskly, 'We're getting more than the usual number of calls requesting home visits—flu cases, more than we can cope with. All the doctors' lists are full. We'll have to do something about it fast.'

He frowned and stared at her blankly, almost as if he didn't understand, then said irritably, 'Rubbish, always manage somehow. Go and discuss it with Tom—he'll come up with an idea. I've got things to do.' He waved a shaky, dismissive hand toward the door and turned back to his desk.

Miranda was dismayed by his seeming indifference to the problem—it was so out of character. Whatever he said, he was clearly unwell and didn't look fit enough to be on duty. That's all we need, she thought ruefully as she made her way along the corridor to the duty room used for emergency appointments, a stricken head of practice *and* a crisis looming.

Her heart beat fast when she reached the emergency room, acutely conscious that Tom was there. She paused outside for a moment, waiting for her quickening heartbeat to subside, before rapping firmly on the half-open door.

'May I come in?' she asked.

There was a little pause then he answered, sounding cool and preoccupied, 'Please do.'

She had hoped for a warmer greeting and had to fight down a little flicker of disappointment. Ridiculous! They were at work. Of course he was preoccupied. He had plenty to think about, and she was going to add to his difficulties.

'Sorry to interrupt,' she said quietly as she slipped into the room, 'but we've got a problem, and Dr Withers suggested that I talk to you about it.'

He looked up from the medical record card that he was filling in and, to her surprise and delight, gave her a sudden glowing, intimate smile that took her breath away. 'Don't be sorry, Miranda, it's good to see you,' he said softly. 'And what's one more problem? Sit down and tell me about it.'

Miranda perched herself on the edge of the patient's chair beside the desk. She forced herself to be matter-of-fact. 'Well, it's not one problem but two—one, the number of home visits being requested and two, Dr Withers.'

Tom leaned on the desk and clasped his hands under his chin. His manner was now completely professional, eyes bright and alert as he looked at her over the top of his specs.

'Explain the problem with visits first.'

'All the doctors' lists are full. It's impossible to cram any more into the regular visiting times after morning or evening surgeries, and loads of patients are ringing in reporting flu symptoms. I'm afraid it does rather look as if we've got a mini-epidemic on our hands, though hopefully a lot of these will be mild cases.'

For a few moments Tom stared at the blank screen

of the VDU in front of him, then he turned to Miranda. 'Right,' he said firmly, 'here's what we do. I'll take over Bill's afternoon surgery—I know he'll be agreeable—and he can concentrate on doing visits. All flu cases to be referred to him; he'll sort the wheat from the chaff and decide who needs follow-up treatment and who can get by just on bed-rest.'

'And what about the emergency surgery? You're down to cover that all day.'

'I'll sandwich it in with Bill's booked-in patients, but everyone should be warned that they might be in for a long wait—it'll be up to Pat and her team to do that diplomatically. We don't want a patient riot on our hands.'

'Don't worry, Pat will sort that out and most people will understand if the situation's explained to them. And I can syphon off patients with minor ailments who are willing to see a nurse. I can fit them in with my usual case load. After all, many of them would end up in the treatment room for dressings and so on under normal circumstances. Trust me, Tom, please. I won't exceed my brief.'

She didn't quite know why it was *so* important that he trust her judgement to deal with patients directly, instead of by referral, but it was. It had something to do with trust in her as a person as well as a professional.

He looked at her thoughtfully for a moment and then said quietly, reaching out across the corner of the desk to touch her arm, 'Of course I trust you, Miranda, implicitly—in every way. And I'm perfectly happy for you to deal with patients directly, but call on me if you have problems or are doubtful about anything—promise.'

'I promise.'

It was like a vow. In complete accord, they smiled into each other's eyes and wordlessly, tenderly, surveyed each other. A wave of perfect harmony flowed between them, engulfing them and eddying round them, until Tom, in gravelly tones, broke into the breathless timeless moment, 'Now, about Dennis,' he said.

Miranda composed herself, found her voice and said matter-of-factly, 'I'm worried about him; he's worse than he was this morning. He shouldn't be working. He hasn't got a surgery this afternoon, just a couple of private insurance examinations. He could go home.'

'Right, leave it with me. I'll see if I can persuade him to pack it in for the day, but I'll sort things out with Bill first.' He picked up the internal phone and slanted her a wicked grin. 'Now, go about your business, woman,' he said, his eyes full of humour but dark with longing too, 'before I ravish you.'

'Is that what you want to do?' she asked, deliberately teasing as she blew him a kiss from the doorway.

'You'd better believe it,' he said huskily as she closed the door. 'At the first opportunity.'

Miranda's heart soared. So this was what love was all about—this sensational feeling, this euphoria, this feeling of oneness that had, till now, eluded her.

Her feet hardly touched the ground as she made her way along the corridor. She had to remind herself that it was going to be a hell of a busy day, and she must concentrate on priorities.

The first thing she did when she returned to her office was to put Pat Payne in the picture about dealing with requests for visits, explaining that Bill Jones would be doing an afternoon list.

'What a relief,' said Pat. 'They're still coming through thick and fast.'

Then she arranged for one of the nurses, Moira Morgan, to visit a nearby rest-home and a sheltered housing unit and give anti-flu injections.

'And check out the chest and heart cases who,

according to their history, might be subject to viral or bacterial problems and are on routine medication,' she advised Moira. 'If they've got scripts for antibiotics suggest they get them in-house, and impress upon them the need to take them at the first sign of any infection. That could prevent all sorts of problems later.'

At twelve o'clock she snatched a belated cup of coffee with Liz, who had been on general duties doing bloods and routine injections, and updated her on the morning's events.

'If this does turn out to be an epidemic,' said Liz, 'aren't we going to be snowed under with requests for anti-flu jabs, even if there's less than a fifty-fifty chance of them being effective so late in the day?'

'I'm sure there will be. We'll tackle that when the time comes—if it comes. Meanwhile, we must encourage the most vulnerable to have jabs, so anyone elderly, chesty or with a circulatory problem should be vaccinated immediately if they're willing.'

'Well, I'll see enough of those this afternoon. I'm on the asthma clinic with our Dr Brent—she'll want to do most of them. I'd better go and get things organised—it looks like being a long session.'

She stood up and walked across the room. At the door she paused and said in a rather subdued voice, 'By the way, about last night, I went a bit over the top. It was the beer. I didn't have much, but I just can't take alcohol. Sorry if I was out of line.'

It was embarrassing to see the usually ebullient Liz so subdued. Miranda said reassuringly, 'Don't worry about it; it's over and done with. Now vanish—we've both got stacks to do.'

Liz had only just left when there was a sharp rap at the door, and Tom appeared.

Before Miranda could open her mouth to speak he crossed the room in a few long strides and—with hands wide apart—leaned on the front of her desk, glaring down at her. She could see that he was both angry and anxious, his well-marked eyebrows drawn together in a ferocious frown.

'I can't bloody well believe it,' he said. 'The man's impossible.'

'Who?' She wanted to smooth away the tortured frown.

'Dennis. He refuses to go home. He's finished his surgery, I've assured him that his afternoon people will be seen but nothing will shift him. And he looks so ill—what the hell am I going to do?'

'Get Val or Bill to back you up; he might listen if you take re-enforcements.'

'They're both out on calls, but he might just listen to you, Miranda. He thinks a hell of a lot of you. Do come and see what you can do.'

'Of course, if you think it will help, but he wouldn't listen to me earlier.'

'Come and try again; let's both grovel. I'd do anything to get the old boy to see sense and go home to bed. The trouble is that since his wife died he hates going home, though he's got a super housekeeper who's been with him for years and would love to spoil him rotten if he'd agree to take a rest for a few days. And he's got a sister in Blandford, who would happily keep him company.' He looked thoughtful. 'Perhaps we could get in touch with her.'

What a kind, generous man he is, thought Miranda. He's so concerned about crusty old Dr Withers; he really cares. It's yet another side of his character that he keeps hidden under that austere exterior.

'Right, then, let's go,' she said softly, 'and see if we can persuade him to see sense.'

'Well, if anyone can, you can,' said Tom, holding open the door for her.

She caught a whiff of astringent cologne as she slid past him, and itched to run her fingers round his firm jaw.

As they walked down the corridor Tom said gruffly, 'Use your special brand of witchery on the old boy, Miranda, love—that should do the trick.'

But it was too late for tricks, they discovered when they reached Dr Withers's room.

Tom knocked twice on the door and, when he didn't receive a reply, opened it.

The doctor was slumped down half in and half out of his chair. His eyes were open but unfocused, his face contorted—head lolling to the left and saliva dribbling from his slack mouth. Almost certainly he'd had a stroke or suffered some sort of brain damage that had affected his left side.

Tom swore savagely, strode across the room and crouched down in front of him. Cupping the pathetically lolling head with firm hands, he straightened it carefully, and peered into the ravaged face. 'Dennis, it's Tom. Can you hear me?'

There was a gurgling sound in Dennis's throat. Was he trying to speak? Miranda crouched at his right side and took hold of his good hand. 'Dr Withers, squeeze my hand if you can hear.'

Nothing happened. Miranda shook her head at Tom. He fished a pencil torch from breast pocket and shone it into Dennis's eyes. There was no reaction.

'Let's get him onto the couch and make him as comfortable as possible,' he said through tight lips.

Together they lifted the heavy, floppy body onto the examination couch, propping him up and turning him slightly on one side to keep his airways clear. Miranda covered the inert figure with a blanket and mopped up the saliva that was tricking from his slack lips.

'Hospital?' she mouthed.

Tom nodded and was silent for a moment as he stood, looking down at his elderly colleague. Then, feeling for the doctor's right wrist, he took his radial pulse. He pulled a face. 'Feeble, erratic,' he murmured. 'Should take his BP, but I see no point in disturbing him; the paramedics can monitor that.'

He bent down and spoke distinctly into Dennis's ear. 'Dennis, you've had a stroke. You'll have to go into hospital for assessment and tests, but they'll soon get you sorted out.'

Grim-faced, he looked at Miranda. 'Buzz Pat to phone for an ambulance, then get me a line to the hospital and I'll speak to the consultant on duty in A and E.' He was abrupt and business like. 'Get hold of Val as soon as he returns; you and he will have to sort things out. He'll have to take over my chores until I get back. I'm going to the hospital with Dennis.'

CHAPTER EIGHT

HALF an hour later Dr Withers, still unconscious, was loaded into the ambulance at the side door of the building and driven away out of sight of patients coming and going by the front entrance.

Val and Miranda watched from the porched doorway as Tom followed the ambulance in his Range Rover. His face was stern, sad. Miranda wanted to hug him, reassure him, he looked so alone and, so vulnerable.

She shivered, but not with cold—though it was still overcast, grey and chilly as it had been early that morning when she had jogged to work. This morning seemed a lifetime away.

Val put a hand under her elbow. 'Let's go in,' he said gently, 'and sort out what we can from this mess.'

They moved back inside the door and, side by side both struggling to suppress a rising tide of consternation at the thought of the difficulties which lay ahead—walked silently along the corridor.

They stopped outside her office and faced each other.

Val put his hands on her shoulders and said wryly, 'Well, this is it, Miranda, love. Things look a bit grim, don't they? A threatened epidemic, a seriously sick head of practice and no Tom temporarily—and Bill out visiting all afternoon. We'd better sort out a new battle plan.' He looked at his watch. 'It's nearly one. I've got phone calls to make. See you here at half past, and we can talk before the doors open at two.'

Making an enormous effort and holding back a wave of apprehension which threatened to engulf her, she said evenly, 'I'll organise sandwiches and coffee, and we can eat at the same time.'

Val grinned. 'There speaks my beautiful and practical Miranda,' he said, and added wistfully, 'God, how I envy the guy who...' He broke off, bent his head, kissed her hard on her forehead and marched away down the corridor.

By the time she met up with Val at one-thirty she had regained her usual cool, and was ready with a few ideas about how to tackle the afternoon's workload.

'Helen's going to stay on and help me in the general duty clinic. Between us we should be able to deal with many of the emergency cases, or at least get a history if they need to see a doctor—that'll save you a bit of time. And they don't have to see you—anyone can see them if they've got a gap. Do you agree?'

'Of course; makes sense. Not that there are going to be many gaps for any of us by the time we each take our share of Bill's patients, as well as our own, but I daresay we'll manage. There'll be, what, five of us doing surgeries?'

'Only four—you, Stella, Leigh and our learner. He's slow, but coping well. Kay's got her asthma clinic and Lydia's on country surgeries.'

Val stared at her in comic dismay. 'Bloody hell, how the devil am I going to fit in those insurance check-ups of Dennis's, do my own list and the emergencies and see my share of Bill's patients? It just ain't possible, lady,' he said in a mock film gangster voice.

'It's all right,' she soothed quickly. 'I've postponed one of Dr Withers's patients and am trying to reach the other but, if I can't, he's not due till three-thirty and Tom might be back by then. He'll come as soon as he can—he knows how much we need him.'

'Well, bless you for getting one of them off my back,

but I shouldn't count on Tom being back too soon. He's not going to leave Dennis on his own.'

'He won't be on his own. His housekeeper will be there, and his sister will be with him shortly. I phoned her earlier and she's coming over from Blandford and will stay as long as necessary. Surely Tom will feel free to return then.'

'It'll depend on how Dennis is doing. He'll feel duty-bound to be with him, if possible, when he recovers consciousness.'

'Duty-bound! I don't understand, Val. I can see that he's fond of Dr Withers and he's worked with him a long time, but so have you. And I can appreciate that he felt he owed it to him as head of practice to see him safely installed in hospital, but to stay indefinitely when we're so pressed here seems a bit excessive.'

She paused for a moment, then said contritely, 'Oh, Lord, I don't mean to sound unsympathetic, but it's just that it's so unlike Tom not to put the practice first and, at the end of the day, it would be what Dr Withers would want.'

Val looked into her puzzled, beautiful green eyes and envied Tom with all his heart, for suddenly it came to him like a bolt of lightning that Miranda the untouchable was in love with his best friend! He'd sensed something between them last night, but hadn't been sure what it was. Now he knew. He felt a hollow where his stomach should be.

He stared down in disgust at the half-eaten sandwich in front of him, and pushed it away. How much should he tell her about Tom to explain why he felt compelled to stay at the hospital? How much was he free to say? He said gruffly, 'Tom's got a special relationship with Dennis. He's known him since he was a boy, and his father was Dennis's partner for years.'

'Oh, I see.' There was something else she sensed,

something that Val didn't want to talk about—and it concerned Tom, the private man, the aloof man, the man she was hungry to know more about. Perhaps, if she persisted. . .'But Tom's father—he must be about Dr Withers's age. Has he retired, or is he in practice somewhere else? I've never heard Tom speak of him.'

'His father's dead. Died a long time ago. . .an accident, tragic. . . Tom doesn't like to talk about it. Suffice it to say that the Withers were very kind to him, and Tom feels he owes Dennis.' He stood up and leaned on the desk, and said curtly, 'There, does that answer your question, Miranda?' His eyes, usually twinkling and full of fun, were veiled and enigmatic.

He'd never spoken to her in that tone of voice, and his vehemence surprised her. Why was he so upset—was it on Tom's behalf or on his own? 'Of course.' She touched his hand. 'I'm sorry, Val. I didn't mean to pry.'

'No, of course you didn't.' He pulled his hand from beneath hers.

Was he being sarcastic? Had he guessed how she felt about Tom? Had that hurt him? For once she couldn't read him.

He straightened up and produced a tight smile. 'Now, let's get on with things. You let Reception know how they're to sort out the patients, and I'll let Lydia and the others know what's happening. . .OK?'

'OK!'

The next couple of hours flew by, leaving her no time to analyse her seething thoughts.

The first person she saw was one of her own booked-in patients, a thin, stressed-out, middle-aged teacher—Mr Little. He was suffering from a painful carbuncle on the back of his neck. The core had been surgically removed, and the open wound had to be redressed with ribbon gauze drainage three times a week. It was a painful procedure and was taking a long time to heal. He seemed so listless, had a bad colour and, though not fat, was unhealthily flabby.

Miranda's heart went out to the man who, two years before, had been reduced to part-time work as a supply teacher. He'd lost his house when he couldn't keep up the mortgage payments, and he and his wife and two children were living in cramped quarters with his in-laws.

She finished the dressing and asked if he was taking his antibiotics regularly.

He confirmed that he was, and added laconically, 'At least I don't have to pay for prescriptions while I'm on income support. But I hate like hell having to depend on hand-outs.' He shrugged his drooping shoulders. 'All I want is to do the job that I'm trained for, earn a modest salary and pay my way.'

Miranda said firmly, 'Free medicine isn't a hand-out—it's what the NHS was created for and you're entitled to it. But you can help yourself by eating properly—that's important when you've got an infection. Are you having plenty of fresh fruit and vegetables?'

Mr Little gave a mirthless laugh. 'Are you kidding?' he said bitterly. 'On my income, with four of us to feed and mother-in-law ruling the kitchen, we're grateful for whatever's put in front of us. Do you know the price of an orange or an apple, Sister?'

'Yes, I do. They're terribly expensive. I'm so sorry—I hadn't thought. One tends to take these things for granted.'

'Yep, like I did until a couple of years ago. You don't appreciate the ripple effect of a breadline income until you experience it. God knows, I was never rich but we could afford decent food and an occasional day out when I was working full time.' He looked at Miranda's lovely, troubled face and said gently, 'Don't worry about it, Sister, we'll survive. Shall I make an appointment for next week on my way out?'

'Please, but come back tomorrow. I'll have a prescription for a vitamin supplement ready for you—that'll help the healing process.' She laid a hand on his shoulder. 'Look, I know it's free and that you'd rather not, but you owe it to yourself and your family to get well as soon as possible.'

His careworn face lit up with a smile. 'You're right. Thanks, Sister, you're a cracker.'

Her next two patients were quickly dealt with and made up for some of the time she'd spent with Mr Little. One was booked in for a regular iron injection and the other for a blood pressure check-up.

She took her fourth Patient from the emergency list—a Mrs Gloria Stone, who was happy to see a nurse.

'It's my waterworks, Sister,' she explained. 'I keep having to spend a penny. It's a nuisance, more than anything. It doesn't hurt, but a friend of mine told me that it can lead to cystitis and I believe that *is* painful.'

'Yes, it's an infection of the bladder that causes inflammation in your front passage—the urethra—and it burns when you pass urine. Frequency is sometimes a forerunner of cystitis, but not always. How long have you had this problem?'

'Two days, I was in and out to the toilet last night, just little dribbles, you know, but I simply had to go. And it was the same at work this morning. I'm not drinking hardly anything, but it hasn't helped.'

'And it won't. In fact, it's the worse thing you can do. You must keep your bladder washed out. It's like flushing out the drains and making sure they don't get silted up. If you get concentrated urine in the bottom of your bladder it irritates it and makes you feel that you must empty it. It can happen when you get dehydrated. Tell me, what sort of work do you do?'

'I'm a hairdresser. It does get pretty hot in the salon sometimes, especially if there are several perms going on, and then I perspire a bit but I'm used to it—it's never affected me.'

'So I see,' said Miranda, glancing at her notes. 'We don't see you here very often. Just roll up your sleeve and I'll take your blood pressure.' She wrapped the cuff of the sphygmomanometer round Mrs Stone's arm above the elbow and inflated it. Then, slowly deflating it, she listened through the stethoscope to the beat of the blood surging through the brachial artery and read the monitor.

'That's brilliant.' She smiled at the plump, pretty-looking woman opposite. 'Well, you don't look it, but I see that you're forty-seven. Have you had any signs of the menopause yet?'

'You mean hot flushes and that sort of thing?' She shook her head. 'No, never, and my periods are regular. Apart from this waterworks thing, which is making me feel a bit washed-out, I'm fit as a flea.'

'So you're not pregnant?' Miranda teased.

Mrs Stone laughed. 'Do me a favour, Sister—at forty-seven?'

'It has been known.'

'Well, not this lady, I can assure you. I've done my bit. No more nappies and sleepless nights for me. The only patter of tiny feet I want to hear is from my grandchildren when they put in an appearance.'

'Right, then we can rule out pregnancy and the menopause. Have you had an attack of diarrhoea or sickness recently?'

'No.'

'Well, it looks as if it's a case of simple dehydration, caused through heat loss when you were working, which should be put right very quickly by drinking plenty of water. But, to be on the safe side, I want you to come in tomorrow morning for a blood test and bring a urine sample with you. Make an appointment at Reception, and then go home and fill yourself up with fluids.'

'Thanks, Sister, will do.' She grinned. 'Now I must dash for the nearest loo—fast.'

After Mrs Stone had gone, Miranda had a moment to wonder what was happening to Dr Withers. Had he regained consciousness? Would his stroke leave him helpless? If it did, Tom would have to take over as head of practice immediately. How he would hate that—stepping into the shoes of a sick man whom he loved and admired, instead of simply inheriting the position when the old doctor retired.

She recalled his reaction when they had discovered the doctor slumped in his chair, and the grim anguish on his face when he had driven after the ambulance. The bond between him and the older man was certainly very strong, and was only partly explained by Val's explanation. Her intuition told her that there was a deeper reason behind Tom's affection for Dr Withers.

She gave herself a mental shake and concentrated on work. There were patients waiting to be seen.

Her own booked-in cases were easy to deal with, a known quantity, mostly changes of wound dressings, prescribed injections and routine diet and weight check-ups and advice.

The emergencies were an unknown factor. Many were straightforward minor problems that she could deal with on the spot, but quite a few had to be passed on to a doctor for assessment and prescriptions for immediate medication, and they simply had to wait their turn.

Some grumbled but, since they had been informed on arrival that there would be a long wait, they resigned themselves to the situation. They could see for themselves that the staff were under pressure, and when it leaked out that Dr Withers had been taken to hospital most were positively sympathetic toward the overworked doctors and nurses.

At some point Pat phoned Miranda to tell her that she had been able to put off the second insurance check-up client.

'That's brilliant, Pat,' she said, and as soon as she had the chance made her way to Val's room to give him the good news.

She caught him between patients.

'Thank God for small mercies,' he said forcefully. 'This afternoon's no joke, but it would have been infinitely worse without your help, Miranda. Thanks. And I'm sorry about our little spat earlier. Am I forgiven?'

'Of course, I shouldn't have pried.'

'Friends.' He smiled and held out his hand, and his hazel eyes were warm and friendly as usual.

She put her hand into his. 'We've done this before,' she said, 'remember?'

He nodded. 'I'm not likely to forget,' he murmured as he slowly released her hand, 'and, don't worry, I'll stick by the rules, Miranda.'

'I know you will,' she said quietly, and turned and left the room.

The long, busy afternoon session was beginning to tail off when Tom appeared in the doorway of the treatment room.

'Can you spare a minute?' he asked in a curiously flat voice.

Miranda, bending over the side bench where she was filling in a treatment card, stifled a gasp of surprise—and a little thread of fear. He sounded so strange; had the worst happened? She looked up. His face was drawn, shuttered.

'How. . .how is he?'

'Conscious, just about; he had another vascular episode in the ambulance. It looks like a haemorrhage, rather than an embolism or thrombosis, but the consultant won't commit himself till the tests have been completed. They're doing a scan right now.'

He walked slowly across the room and sank heavily onto a chair. 'Poor old Dennis, it's hell seeing him like this. Even if he does pull through, what sort of future does he have? This is a big one, Miranda, and likely to leave him paralysed and helpless.'

She couldn't bear the hopelessness in his voice and the bleakness in his eyes. He was no longer the competent doctor but the loving anxious friend, needing reassurance.

She took a deep breath and said briskly, 'Not necessarily. There might be only minimal damage. Strokes are notoriously difficult to assess—you know that. He could make an almost complete recovery.'

Hope flickered in his eyes. 'Do you think so?'

'Yes.'

'It would be a miracle if he did.'

'Miracles happen. We've both seen them; we've talked about it before.' She touched his slumped shoulder. 'Tom, don't sound so despairing; it's not like you.'

Abruptly he straightened his shoulders and stood up. A faint smile curled up his mouth at one corner. 'What you mean is stop feeling sorry for yourself and get on with some work.'

She murmured softly, 'Something like that and, heaven knows, there's plenty to do.'

'Then I'd better get stuck in. What's the state of play?'

'There are still a number of emergencies to be seen and several booked-in patients. If you could take over some of those it will speed things up.'

'Right, I'll go and have a word with Val and put him in the picture about Dennis. You can let the others know what's happening. And ask Pat to send in the rest of the emergencies to me.' He moved to the door. 'And, thanks, Miranda, for holding the fort and everything,' he said as he stepped into the corridor.

'It's my job,' she said simply.

'And then some,' he said, and walked away down the corridor.

The afternoon surgeries merged into the early evening sessions, and it was well after six before Miranda was able to escape to her office.

Her in-tray was full of slips of paper left by the medical staff, recording the number of flu patients they had treated during the day. Bill had seen eleven cases, the others four or five cases each. She collated them and faxed the aggregate number through to County Hall. Considering that this was just the tip of the iceberg and that there must be many unreported cases, it was clear that they had an embryo epidemic on their hands.

She was still mulling over this unpleasant conclusion and replanning the off-duty to cover a heavier workload when Val looked in to say goodnight.

'I'm starting on my evening calls. I'm on till ten,' he said, 'then Tom takes over. So I'll see you in the morning, sweetie, no doubt looking your usual radiant, beautiful self. But, before I go, I just wanted to say thanks for everything you've done today, keeping us on our toes and getting us organised. We couldn't have managed without you.'

'Rubbish, Val, don't exaggerate. You were a tower of strength and everyone pulled their weight—combined effort. We make a good team.'

He grinned. 'The Dunkirk spirit and all that.'
'Exactly.'

Miranda was still working on the charts about half an hour later when Tom appeared. He stood just inside the room, one broad shoulder propped against the doorjamb.

'I thought you'd like to know the latest on Dennis. I've just rung the hospital.'

His voice was flat, expressionless. Fear knocked at her heart. 'And. . .?'

'They've confirmed a left side cerebral haemorrhage. It's not as massive as it might have been, though they have warned that there could be another. And he's regained full consciousness, though at the moment he's sedated so there's no question of visiting tonight. I'm almost afraid to believe it, but matters do look fractionally better than they did this afternoon.'

He pushed himself away from the doorjamb and gave her a quirky, gentle smile. 'You were right, dear heart. One should never give up hope,' he said quietly.

Her pulse raced, her mouth went dry—*dear heart*, and said with such tenderness. 'No, one shouldn't. I'm so glad, Tom.' She returned his smile. 'Are you going now?' she asked, just managing to keep a quiver out of her voice.

'In about ten minutes. What about you?'

'I've still masses to do.'

He strode across the room and leaned on the desk, looking down at her, his dark eyes raking her face. 'Miranda, my love, it's after seven, and for the first time today the waiting-room's empty. You're going to shut up shop, and that's an order. I'll be back for you in ten minutes.'

How masterful! How ferociously masculine! And how she loved him. The worst of the difficult day was over. Relief flooded over her. She wanted to giggle—to tease him. Her eyes shone. She lifted her chin.

'Thanks, but I'll walk home. I usually do.'

'My dear good girl, you'll do no such thing. You've had a helluva day and it's nearly dark.'

'I don't mind walking in the dark.'

'But I mind very much.'

'Do you?' She arched her beautifully marked brows.

He saw through her, and chuckled. 'Don't tease, Miranda.' Glimmering brown eyes met lambent sea-green eyes for an instant, then he stood up abruptly and made for the door. 'Back in ten minutes. Be ready.'

There was little traffic about as they drove smoothly through the gathering dusk along the one-way system circling the cathedral.

Sitting beside Tom, Miranda felt wonderfully content—quietly happy. She couldn't describe it, but she felt warm, glowing vibes flowing between them. She felt that she had known him for ever. She knew that she could say anything to him and that he would understand. Was this what loving was all about? She stared up at the three sturdy towers etched against the darkening sky.

'It's so homely,' she murmured. 'I love it. It makes me feel that I belong, even though I've been here such a short while. Does that sound weird or affected?'

'No. It's the still, calm centre of Combe Minster, and I've known it all my life and I feel that way about it too.'

They paused at traffic lights.

'I go in sometimes and just sit and pray and think,' said Miranda softly.

'I know. I do the same. I saw you the other evening, but you weren't sitting. You were kneeling, very straight-backed, like a statue.' He glinted a sideways smile at her.

Miranda chuckled. 'Legacy of my convent school-days. But I didn't see you.'

'I was the other side of the aisle and behind you. I left before you did. I had an evening surgery.'

'I stayed for Evensong.'

'I thought you might.'

Nothing had been said about love, but Miranda felt that in some subtle way they were speaking of love. But perhaps that was all nonsense and it was simply what she wanted to believe.

They reached Almond Terrace, and Tom pulled up before number five. For some unaccountable reason she felt suddenly shy and gauche, like a schoolgirl on her first date—not a sophisticated beautiful woman.

Her heart pounding, she asked, 'Would you like to come in for coffee?' He hadn't been inside the cottage since the day she had arrived. Surely he would say yes.

He shook his head. 'No, thanks, Miranda. Much as I'm tempted, I won't. I've got to get home, walk Henry, have a bite to eat and then get my head down for an hour or so. I'm on call from ten, and something tells me that it's going to be a busy night. I'll need to be on top of things.'

Of course he had to; it made sense. He'd been on the go all day. But just a little longer in his company! She clutched at a straw. 'I could rustle you up something to eat while you walk Henry. That would save time.'

'Pinky will have prepared something.'

Her heart almost stopped. 'Pinky?'

'I don't keep fairies at the bottom of my garden; I keep Pinky, my cordon bleu housekeeper. She lives in a flat over the garage in a converted stable block.'

'Oh,' Miranda said breathlessly. Housekeepers, especially super, cordon bleu housekeepers, came in all sorts of shapes and sizes—willowy blondes, bouncing brunettes, ravishing redheads. She let her imagination run riot. 'That must be convenient,' she added in a whispery sort of voice.

Tom said with a throaty chuckle, 'She's a lovely lady—sixtyish, and has a devoted husband who's a retired civil servant. He's a keen gardener and potters around, keeping my little plot in order.' He took her hands in his and his eyes, full of gentle humour, looked steadfastly into hers.

She said indignantly, 'You were winding me up.'

'Yes.'

'Why?'

He took a deep breath. He'd have to take the plunge. What did it mattered if he revealed himself? 'I wanted to see if, by any remote chance, you cared enough to mind that I might be involved with another woman.'

'And. . .?'

'I think you do care—just a little. Don't you, Miranda?'

Was this the moment to throw discretion to the wind; to tell him that she'd been in love with him for months; that she'd never loved like this before, and that it was a totally new experience for her?

And did *he* care, or was he just superficially attracted to her? Could she trust the vibes that seemed to flow between them or the kisses he had showered upon her this morning? Or were they the smooth foreplay of the sophisticated confirmed bachelor out for a killing?

Her heart shrivelled with pain. 'Do *you* care, Tom?' she asked in a quivering voice.

His eyebrows came together in a frown. 'Of *course* I bloody care. Isn't it obvious?'

She shook her head.

'Then perhaps this'll convince you.' He dropped her hands, gripped her shoulders and, pulling her to him, planted a long, hard, savage kiss on her slightly parted lips.

Making a little mew of surprise and pain, Miranda struggled for a few moments to pull away from him. Then suddenly she stopped struggling—she wanted the kiss to go on for ever. She slid her hands round his waist, pressed him even closer and gave herself up to the probing of his hard, muscular tongue as it explored the moist, warm depths of her mouth.

And when he gently withdrew his tongue she nibbled at his lip and drew blood. She teased at it with the tip of her own tongue, revelling in its warm saltiness.

He lifted his head. He was breathing deeply, his eyes glinting in the amber light of the streetlamp. He was still grasping her aching shoulders and pressing his solid chest against her soft breasts.

'Now,' he rumbled huskily, 'do you believe that I care and that I want you desperately?'

'I do,' she said softly, running her tongue over her bruised lips.

'Good, now we know where we stand.' He released her shoulders and, leaning across her, opened the passenger door. 'Now go, woman, please, before I make a complete ass of myself.' He brushed a kiss across her cheek and gave her a gentle push toward the door.

'Goodnight, dearest love. Sleep well; happy dreams,' he said as she stepped down onto the pavement. 'And gird your loins for a busy day tomorrow. See you in the morning, bright and early.' Then smoothly letting in the clutch, he drove off.

'See you,' she whispered, feeling bereft because he was leaving her. But there was tomorrow. The thought gave her some comfort as she watched the tail-lights of the car disappear down the street.

* * *

In fact, she didn't see him bright and early as he'd promised—he was still out on a call when she arrived at the surgery.

But he phoned in on his mobile just before eight. He greeted her warmly, his voice low and vibrant and sending a shiver up her spine. 'Morning, my love. All well with you?'

Did he mean had she recovered from that all-consuming kiss? She said softly, breathlessly, trying to invest the mundane words with a deeper meaning and wishing that she could say boldly, I love you, 'Yes, *I'm* fine. Tom. And *you*?'

'Bit weary. Had a hectic night, but I'm on my way home now to shower and change and grab some breakfast. Be with you by nine to take Dennis's surgery; good job I've got a late start with mine.'

She said fiercely, 'You should have a rest.'

'Concerned about me, Miranda?' His voice was silky.

'You know I am. You had a dreadful day yesterday.'

'Letting your heart for once rule that cool head of yours?'

Why pretend? 'Yes, I rather think I am.'

There was a long pause then he said, his voice very deep, 'You've no idea how happy that makes me.' And added briskly, 'Now I must go; see you anon.'

He switched off and the link with him was broken.

Carefully Miranda replaced the receiver as if it was something precious. Her heart was thumping painfully and she felt light-headed. It was unbelievable—just his voice did incredible things to her.

She cleared her throat and swallowed hard. 'Pull yourself together, woman,' she muttered. 'You've stacks to do. Put Tom out of your mind and concentrate on work; it looks like being a busy day.'

CHAPTER NINE

THE rest of the day was one mad rush as requests for anti-flu vaccination soared when it became generally known through the media that the county was in the throes of an epidemic.

Miranda set aside one of the treatment rooms to function as an anti-flu clinic, with Liz in charge to deal with the flood of patients turning up for jabs.

'And please make it plain to everyone, Liz, that they may already be infected, in which case the vaccine's not going to help. So many people seem to think that it's a miracle cure, not just a preventative.'

She gave the same advice to another nurse, whom she sent out on home visits to deal with vaccinations for their most vulnerable housebound patients.

With two nurses short, she had to manage the general duties clinic single-handed and shelve all her own admin work until the evening.

She didn't see Tom until midmorning when he brought news that he'd been in touch with the hospital and learned that Dennis was stable, though still critically ill.

'I'll try to visit him briefly this afternoon when out on calls,' he said, speaking from the door of the treatment room as she was labelling up specimen bottles.

Miranda glanced across at him, her lovely face full of compassion. 'Tell him we're all rooting for him, and he's not to worry about the practice. Everything's going smoothly. That's what he'll want to hear.'

'Will do,' he promised, raising a tired smile and drinking in her radiant beauty.

She wanted to kiss his drooping mouth and smooth the creases in his forehead. Resolutely she turned her attention back to the bench to keep her hands busy, her head bent over the bottles.

He asked in a low voice, 'Did you mean what you said this morning—about letting your heart ruling your head?'

Without looking up, she said softly, 'I did.'

In three easy strides he crossed the room, removed a bottle from her grasp, placed it on the work top and turned her round. He took her hands in his and pinioned them behind her back, pressing her close and forcing her to tilt back her head and look up at him.

His breathing was ragged and his dark, glittering eyes searched her face. 'Do you love me, Miranda?' he asked fiercely. 'Really love me?'

For endless moments she held her breath until it hurt. This was it—the moment of truth. She couldn't keep it back any longer, and why should she? Slowly she expelled the long-held breath and said, 'Yes,' on a whisper.

She waited for him to kiss her, embrace her, murmur words of love but, to her utter surprise and dismay, he did none of those things but continued to gaze down at her in silence.

He said at last, 'That's what I wanted to hear. I've cracked the ice.' There was quiet satisfaction in his voice. He released her hands suddenly and took a step backwards before he said, 'I'll take you home tonight. We've a helluva lot of catching up to do; we've wasted so much time.' And, turning smartly, he walked toward the door.

The arrogance of the man. He was triumphant, victorious. How could he walk away from her without a kiss, having coerced her into admitting her love for him? He hadn't said that he loved her, not in so many words. It wasn't enough that he had made it crystal clear that he was glad that she loved him. She wanted to hear him say, '*I love you*,' and mean it.

She quelled anger and all sorts of emotions, and said airily, 'Oh, I don't think so, not tonight. I'll make my own way home. I'll be working late—stacks to do.'

He shed his tiredness and grinned from the doorway, one of his quirky, lopsided grins. 'It doesn't matter how late, dear heart. I've stacks to do too,' he said jauntily. 'Just let me know when you're ready,' and with that he was gone.

Damn the man. He took her breath away with his haughtiness, his certainty that she would comply with his wishes. Yet he had called her 'dear heart', as if he'd meant it—a rather touching, quaint, old-fashioned phrase full of tenderness. She clung to the thought.

Making a determined effort to put her meeting with Tom—and its mood swings—behind her, she set about concentrating on work for the rest of the day. It wasn't too difficult; there was so much to do. She drank coffee and ate half a sandwich in between doing blood and urine tests and the occasional dressing in the morning and a long list of cervical smears in the afternoon.

She didn't see anything of Tom. He went out on calls after morning surgery and continued them over the afternoon, covering both for himself and Dr Withers.

It was after six when she got back to her office, and the phone rang before she had even sat down at her desk. Tom, she thought, her pulse racing.

It wasn't Tom.

'I've got a Mr Jones on the line from the administrator's department at Combe General,' said the receptionist. 'Wants to speak to you or one of the doctors, but they're all out or busy in their surgeries.'

'Put him through,' said Miranda, squashing her disappointment. When he came on the line she said,

'What can I do for you, Mr Jones?'

'Well, the short answer is don't send in any more patients for a bit.'

'Good heavens, why not?'

'Because we're short of beds, and getting short of nursing staff. You'd be amazed at the number who've already gone off sick with this bug.'

'I'm *not* amazed,' replied Miranda caustically. 'They're overworked and, like most hospitals, you're always understaffed on the wards. I'm not surprised that they're dropping like flies.'

There was a muffled exclamation at the other end and, realising that she was probably ruffling administrative feathers—which wasn't a good idea—added diplomatically, 'Look, I know it's not your fault, Mr Jones, but it puts us in a rotten position, doesn't it, not being able to hospitalise patients when necessary?'

Somewhat mollified, Mr Jones said, 'You could try hospitals further afield. Some area hospitals may not be as pushed as we are.'

'Thanks,' said Miranda drily, 'we'll do that. Goodnight.'

The news was greeted with dismay by the doctors when she buzzed each of them to put them in the picture, and with hoots of derision when she passed on the suggestion that they tried other hospitals.

Tom, just back from his extended calls, said bitterly, 'Every other medic in the county will be doing the same. There just won't be enough beds to go round. What do we do with our coronaries, suspect appendix, and so on? Any bright ideas, my clever Miranda?'

She was warmed, exhilarated by his mild praise—*his* clever Miranda.

'We've got some good private nursing homes in the area; we could use those, if our accountants will agree. Medical beds won't cost more, if as much, as they would in hospital, though some of the surgical facilities might. I could find out what's available and reserve some beds, though it will cost us.'

'Do it; we'll talk funding later. And we'll have a meeting at nine after evening surgeries and clinics. I know everyone will be flat out—it's been a hectic day—but we've got to get our priorities sorted out. How to cope with our routine work and take care of the critical flu cases. Some of those I've seen this afternoon are pretty ropy, and I'm worried about side-effects.'

'I'll round everyone up and lay on snacks and coffee.'

'Brilliant, love, I knew I could depend on you.'

By the time the meeting ended it was after ten, but they had thrashed out a working agenda.

The Well Woman's and Well Man's clinics and the weights and blood pressure clinics were to be suspended for the time being. Patients needing special care were to be admitted to local private nursing homes. Those in need of intensive care who couldn't be accommodated in the county hospitals would be shipped across the border into Hampshire, as yet unaffected by the epidemic.

'It will be your job each morning, Miranda,' said Tom, giving her a secret, tender smile, 'to suss out which hospitals have beds.'

'Will do,' she said tranquilly, happy because he had smiled at her and making a note in her already full notebook.

It was decided that two doctors should be on call until two a.m. each night to cover escalating demand, then one doctor would be on call for the rest of the night. Everyone would continue to cover Dr Wither's list. And the practice physiotherapist would be asked to make domiciliary visits to treat patients with chest complications in their own homes.

For the second night Tom and Miranda drove home round the amber-lit one-way system circumnavigating the cathedral at the heart of the city. But tonight they were silent, deep in thought, bone-weary yet vitally aware of each other.

Miranda fluttered a hand toward Almond Terrace as they drove past.

Tom ignored the gesture. 'You must be sick of scratch meals. I'm taking you home for something hot,' he said. 'I asked Pinky to leave a casserole for two in the oven.'

She sat up straight. 'So you planned all this before I'd agreed to let you drive me home,' she spat out angrily. 'Well, I'm poleaxed, Tom, I want an early night. Don't think that because I—'

'Said you loved me I can have my wicked way with you?' His voice was teasing but infinitely gentle. He shook his head. 'Dismiss the thought. I'm just offering you supper, Miranda—no strings. I don't plan to seduce you.' He pulled a wry face and then grinned. 'Apart from anything else, I'm knackered. I couldn't do you justice.'

His male ego was at stake. Her anger fled, and she slanted a smile at him. 'So I'm quite safe,' she said softly.

'Quite.'

They pulled up outside his charming Regency house, which she had passed and admired many times. He released his seat belt and then Miranda's.

'Out you get, dear girl,' he said, 'we're home.'

Henry barked distantly as Tom fitted his key into the shining black front door, and when they entered the elegant square hall he padded across the black and white tiled floor to greet them joyously.

They fussed over him for a moment then, taking her by the elbow, Tom steered Miranda to a room at the back of the hall. 'We're eating in here,' he said, opening the door. 'Pinky will have put the food on the hot plate and wine in the cooler, so let's enjoy a decent meal. I think we deserve it after the bloody awful day that we've had.'

Carefully, as if she might break, he sat her down at the round polished table in the small, beautifully proportioned room with white panelled walls which, for all its elegance, had a homely, lived-in feel.

'I thought a light, dry wine,' he said, standing at her side and filling her glass with crystal clear liquid.

Miranda sniffed and took a sip. 'Lovely,' she pronounced. She felt light-headed, as if she was floating on air. It was all unreal being here with Tom in his house—it was out of this world. She took a deep breath, hoping that she wasn't going to faint.

He sat down on the opposite side of the table, leaned over and touched his full glass to hers. 'Welcome to my home, Miranda,' he murmured softly. 'I've waited a long time for this moment.'

'Thank you,' she whispered. Her hand trembled.

He looked at her pale face and huge eyes. 'You must eat,' he said abruptly, 'or you'll faint—low blood sugar. You didn't eat anything this evening, only drank black coffee.'

He served her with a huge helping of a rich, spicy chicken casserole with saffron rice and vegetables. They ate in hungry, companionable silence for a while, and Henry lay at Tom's feet and snored softly.

'This was once the card room,' explained Tom a little later, when their first hunger assuaged. He ladled more chicken and rice on to her plate. 'I use it for intimate dinner parties; the dining-room proper is a bit large and over-elegant.'

'*Intimate* dinner parties?'

His eyes gleamed, and he grinned. 'Not intimate, in the sense you mean,' he said smoothly. 'Just a few friends for a meal and intelligent conversation. Before I got caught up in this tennis tournament marathon I did quite a bit of entertaining.'

'So I believe.' She forked up another mouthful of food. 'How are you going to fit in tennis, with so much going on in the practice?'

'I'm not going to try. It's impossible. I'm going to opt out; I know Liz will be disappointed but it can't be helped.'

'She'll understand.'

'I hope so.' He collected up the empty plates. 'Now pudding. Pinky's left us lemon mousse.'

Miranda shook her head. 'Don't think I can manage it. Lord, I'm so tired.' She felt her eyelids drooping.

'A couple of mouthfuls,' he pleaded. 'It'll slide down, and then Henry and I will walk you home.' He smiled into her eyes and swiftly kissed the tip of her nose. 'Good food, some fresh air and you'll sleep like an angel.'

And she did, like a happy, replete, contented baby, knowing that she loved and was loved and confident that she could tackle any difficulties that might lie ahead.

There were certainly plenty of difficulties to meet over the next few weeks.

A minor one was Liz. She was very upset when Tom told her that he couldn't compete in the tennis tournament and turned on Miranda, accusing her of influencing Tom to withdraw.

Miranda, up to her eyes in work, for once was in no mood to go softly, softly.

'Think what you like, Liz,' she said brusquely. 'I had nothing to do with it. It's between you and Tom. Sort it out with him—after all, you're old friends.'

Liz said bitterly, 'And, thanks to you, that's all we are—friends. If you hadn't butted in. . .'

'I didn't butt in, Liz. I don't go around pinching other women's men. As I understand it, Tom's your tennis partner—nothing more.'

Liz's shoulders sagged suddenly and she looked at Miranda with tear-drenched eyes. 'You're right,' she said sadly. 'That's all we've ever been—friends. I won't make waves; I know when I'm beaten. He's all yours, Miranda.' Turning on her heel, she walked stiffly, touchingly dignified, out of the office.

But the major difficulties that had to be dealt with were numerous.

Several flu patients were desperately ill and in need of intensive care, and had to be hospitalised over the county borders. One patient died on the journey, and the media wouldn't be content till Miranda gave an interview and explained why it had been necessary to move the patient to a hospital miles away when there was one on their doorstep.

NO ROOM AT THE INN, OR IN THIS CASE THE LOCAL HOSPITAL, blazed a headline, and the editorial continued, 'Hard-pressed local doctors forced to buy bed care for their patients in neighbouring counties because of shortage of staff at city hospital.'

But it wasn't only the hospital that was short of staff for, in a very short time, practice staff began to succumb to the bug.

For the most part they were only mildly affected and returned to work, pale but determined, within three or four days. But there was one hair-raising period over thirty-six hours when several went off sick before others had returned.

This reduced the staff to four doctors—Tom, Val, Bill and Lydia—and three nurses—Miranda, Liz and Mary Bailey, who came out of retirement to help out.

'You can always rely on the old toughies,' said Val cheerfully, preparing to embark on a horrendous number of crucial visits one morning at the height of the crisis.

What a joy he was to have around, mused Miranda—a trusty colleague and a true friend.

The reception staff were drastically reduced too, leaving Pat Payne and three assistants to field the requests for home visits and sooth prickly patients who had to wait lengthy periods to be seen. But they kept their cool and plodded heroically on, and it became clear that as long as patients were informed as to what was happening they accepted the situation sympathetically.

But everyone had to work flat out. There were no more intimate suppers for Tom and Miranda. In fact, some days they scarcely saw each other. Just occasionally he drove her home when they left the centre together, but they were too weary to do more than drink a mug of coffee, mull over the day's happenings and part with a peck on the cheek.

They both worked from early morning to late at night, keeping things ticking over at the centre, and in addition Tom had to do his share of night duty and head the practice. There was no time for a personal life.

'Some day we'll pick up where we left off,' he said one night, brushing a kiss against her cheek as he dropped her off at Almond Terrace. 'Till then we have to put everything on hold.'

'Promises, promises,' she uttered ruefully to the tail-light of his car as he drove off in answer to a call on his mobile phone. Yet, in a way, the emergency had brought them wonderfully close in a short time. They didn't need words—their eyes, an occasional touch or a fleeting kiss spoke volumes.

Then slowly, almost imperceptibly, over the next couple of weeks things began to return to normal. No fresh flu cases were reported, and one day there was a full complement of staff on duty.

Miranda asked Liz and Pat to come to her office.

'We're back to normal,' she said jubilantly. 'Let's sort out some extra time off for staff who held the fort over the crisis, not forgetting ourselves. We've all earned a break.'

Pat said, 'Any time suits me; I just want to catch up on some sleep. No more stopping till all hours to file records and so on—bliss.'

'Well, I leave it up to you to organise that and other days off in your department; just let me have a list by this evening. I'll sort out the nurses. Now, what about you, Liz? As long as either you or I are on at any one time it doesn't matter how we play it.'

'I'd like to have time off either side of the weekend,' said Liz, 'to go to a friend's wedding and actually socialise.'

'Then I'll go off at five tonight and take tomorrow and the next two days,' said Miranda, 'and, like Pat, enjoy just lazing around.' Her imagination went into overdrive. Perhaps at last Tom and I— She broke off in mid-thought, her heart leaping.

The internal phone rang an hour later. It was Tom. Her heart did its usual acrobatics.

'I've got tonight off,' he said in his deep throaty voice. 'Val and the others insist; seem to think I might fall by the wayside if I don't get a break.'

'They're right. You've been working flat out.'

'So's everybody. We all need a break.'

'You, more than anybody—you carry the heaviest load. We've got to keep you ticking over; the practice needs you, Tom.'

'It needs you too, Miranda, but, by God, I need you more. I'm sick of sharing you with half the population of Combe Minster. They can do without you tonight; it's my turn. Take the evening off, dear girl, and that's an order.' His voice dropped to a menacing growl.

Miranda prickled all over and shivered with pleasure. 'Yes, sir, my lord and master.' Laughter bubbled in her throat. 'I wouldn't dream of disobeying you in this mood.'

'Lady, you ain't seen nothing yet,' he rasped. 'Now, get yourself off duty, go home and put on something stunning—something that's not remotely like a uniform. I'm taking you out for a civilised dinner and then, well, who knows? Pick you up at half-seven.'

He collected her in a taxi. 'So that I can enjoy a drink,' he explained.

They drove out of the city to dine at Peckham Place, an old country house which had been converted into a quietly sumptuous hotel, renowned for its cuisine of simple dishes perfectly cooked and perfectly served.

The *maître d'*, who knew Tom as a regular patron, led them to one of the looped curtained alcoves that opened off the main dining-room. Deftly, reverently, he helped Miranda off with her shimmering black satin evening jacket, before seating her at the table and offering her a snow-white napkin and elegant menu card.

He moved round the table and handed Tom a menu. 'Shall I send the wine waiter, sir?'

'Please.'

Soft-footed, with a lingering glance at Miranda, he went away.

'Thought he'd never go,' growled Tom. 'Damn man nearly ate you, not that I blame him—you look edible, fabulous.' His dark, hungry eyes skimmed her nearly bare shoulders, creamy against the black silk of her dress, and travelled down the plunging deep V which disappeared between the gentle swell of her breasts.

Miranda blushed slightly. Did he think it was too revealing? 'You said wear something unlike a uniform,' she said demurely.

He grinned widely and raised his eyebrows. 'And I can honestly say that I've never seen a uniform like that.' He leaned across the table and stroked his forefinger round her chin. 'Oh, Miranda, I. . .'

The wine waiter arrived to discuss years and vintages. Miranda barely heard a word. She didn't care what they drank—it would all taste like nectar. Surely Tom had been about to say, 'love you'.

The waiter went away.

She slanted a glance at Tom. He was looking across at her.

'Champagne,' he murmured. 'It's the only fitting wine with which to celebrate.'

Her eyes locked with his. 'Are we celebrating?'

'You know we are. End of the scourge, a beginning for us, Miranda, for you and me.'

'A beginning?' Her heartbeat thundered in her ears, and she was conscious of her breasts rising and falling with every breath she took.

A waiter arrived to collect their order, hovering discreetly a little way from the table.

'You choose for me,' she breathed to Tom.

'You might not like what I choose.'

'I will.' Her eyes were shining with love. 'Whatever you choose will be perfect.'

They both knew that they weren't talking about food.

She was giving him carte blanche to choose for the evening and for rest of her life.

The food didn't matter. They didn't know what they ate or drank; it all tasted wonderful. They talked and talked—words, electricity, vitality vibrating between them. They wanted to bare their souls to each other, and exchanged precious, sometimes bitter details about their personal histories.

'My parents died in a car accident,' said Miranda sadly. 'Dad had a heart attack, brought on by anxiety over business. He was in aeronautics. He went bust at the end of the eighties and lost everything. There's just my sister, Juliet, and me left now. She's a bit scatty, but is happily married, has three children and lives in York. We phone each other every week.'

'You mentioned her at your interview.'

'You remember that?'

'I remember everything about that very first day, Miranda, when I saw you for the first time.'

'So do I,' she whispered. 'You looked so stern in your specs.' She paused and then asked, 'And what about you, Tom. Have you got a family?'

His mouth twisted at the corner. 'No, there's just me. I was an only child. My father brought me up when my mother walked out when I was quite small. It was pretty tough for him; he was a busy GP. He and Dennis were partners; the Withers were wonderful friends.'

'Val told me.'

'Did he tell you that my father committed suicide?'

'Oh, no! Oh, my darling, I'm so sorry.' She reached across the table and touched his hand. She longed to give him a comforting hug. 'Why?'

'Because, after all those years, he was still in love with my mother. He waited till I was through med school, then overdosed on morphine. It was grim for the practice, but Dennis weathered it and remained my friend and, when I'd done my hospital stint and some paediatric work, he offered me a partnership.'

'So Dennis is very special to you.'

'Very.' His lips curved into a smile. 'He thinks you're the tops, you know—"a woman of beauty, heart and brains" is how he refers to you. It'll give him a great boost to hear about us.'

Her eyes glittered with sudden tears. 'I'm glad,' she said softly. 'I'm awfully fond of that grumpy old man.'

With a long forefinger Tom gently smoothed a tear-drop from her cheek. 'I know,' he said. 'I'm almost jealous.'

'Good,' she murmured with a chuckle. 'A little competition never hurt anyone.'

At last, drowning in each other's eyes, they talked themselves into a throbbing silence which pulsated across the table.

Tom emptied his brandy glass. 'Let's go home,' he said softly. He didn't need to ask, Your place or mine, but Miranda answered as if he had spoken.

'Mine please, the cottage.' She wanted to give herself to him in her own miniature castle,' she didn't want to share him, even with handsome Henry.

They communicated silently in the back of the taxi, clasping hands, legs pressed close thigh to thigh.

Her lovely long legs were sheathed in sheerest silk! He could picture the curved calf, the slender ankle. Tom felt his heartbeat quicken, his genitals throb and harden. He caressed her palm seductively with his thumb and Miranda sighed and trembled beside him. He exulted in her feminine vulnerability.

She was his.

He had no uncertainties; they were meant for each other. Tonight he was going to make love to her, mad, passionate love—arouse her, make her helpless with desire. The waiting time was over. He was going to marry this beautiful woman, who had entranced him since they'd first met. There was an inevitability about it. Tonight he would propose. Nothing could come between them.

They arrived back at Almond Terrace at eleven-thirty. As Tom paid off the taxi driver a large estate car cruised slowly past and pulled up under the streetlamp a few yards along the road.

Miranda, standing beside Tom on the pavement, froze and then exclaimed in utter amazement, 'That's my sister's car.'

'Your sister? What the devil is she doing here?' Tom ground out.

Miranda mumbled, 'There must be something terribly wrong,' and started to sprint toward the car.

A woman stumbled out of the driver's seat and ran to meet her.

Tom stared in shocked disbelief as they embraced each other, seeing his plans for the evening smashed to smithereens. He wouldn't have his lovely Miranda to himself—he wouldn't be able to make love to her, hold her in his arms and propose to her.

He could scarcely contain the rage and anger that washed through him, frightening in its intensity. He seethed. Then common sense took over. He took several deep breaths and regained control over his raging emotions. As Miranda had said, there must be some sound, possibly serious reason why her sister had turned up late at night without warning.

He composed his features into their usual calm, reassuring mode, squared his shoulders and strode along the pavement to where Miranda stood with her arms about her sister.

Juliet was in floods of tears.

'Is there anything I can do?' he asked. 'Or would you rather I disappeared?'

Miranda's anguished eyes met his over her sister's shoulder. 'Please stay,' she pleaded. 'I'm going to need help with the children.'

'Children?' Of course, there were children.

'In the back of car. . .and, Tom, I'm so sorry, so dreadfully sorry.'

'Not the end of the world,' he said, giving her a wintry smile. 'Now let's see to these children.'

CHAPTER TEN

FOR Tom and Miranda the next hour flew by as they dealt with the two small children, Ben and Daisy—who were glassy-eyed with exhaustion—and a fretful baby Lucy. At last they were all fed and bedded down for the night and Juliet, who had babbled on non-stop while they had been caring for her children, had gone off to take a hot bath.

Tom heaved a sigh of relief. Though outwardly calm, inwardly he had raged at Juliet for destroying their evening and worrying Miranda.

He had gathered from her incoherent chattering that she was leaving her husband, Hugo, because he'd been unfaithful to her. But weren't her tears a little exaggerated, her manner too brittle? Was she really as distressed as she seemed, or was she putting on an act to secure Miranda's sympathy?

Impatiently he squashed the uncharitable thought. It was none of his business, except that it was because Miranda was involved.

Conscious of the tiny cottage being full of people, they didn't linger in the sitting-room when they found themselves at last alone. Looking parchment-pale, but still very beautiful, Miranda saw him to the door.

Tom took her in his arms, and nuzzled her nose. 'Don't let Juliet keep you up till all hours,' he said softly. 'She's on a high. She'll want to talk, but you need your sleep and so does she. Give her brandy and some hot milk and send her to bed. I'll be in after morning surgery, but call me anytime if you need me and I'll be here in a flash.'

Miranda dredged up a tired smile. 'My knight on a white charger,' she whispered.

He chuckled. 'I was thinking more of Superman.'

'Idiot.' Her eyes misted over. She reached up and kissed him softly on the mouth. 'I do love you,' she said. 'I'm so sorry the evening was spoilt.'

'The feeling's mutual,' he murmured, and kissed her back hard and briefly, before releasing her and stepping out into the frosty night. 'Goodnight, my darling, sleep well.'

As Tom had predicted Juliet did want to talk, and Miranda hadn't the heart to stop her.

'Hugo's having an affair with his secretary,' she insisted tearfully. 'It's been going on for months. He's always working late at the office, and now he's gone rushing off to Canada. He *says* it's because he's got to get this contract to save the firm from going bust, but I don't believe him.'

'Why not? Don't you remember how hard Dad worked to try to save his firm? Small businesses go under every day and, as an architect, Hugo must have been affected by the building recession. Give him a break, Juliet. You've got a marvellous marriage; he adores you. Don't spoil it. Talk to him. At least let him know where you are.'

'He knows where I am. I left a message on the answerphone. But, if he rings, I don't want to talk to him. I won't.' Her mouth set in the obstinate line that was only too familiar to Miranda. 'If he loves me he'll come home, whatever happens to the wretched contract.'

'That's blackmail,' said Miranda sharply.

'So?' Juliet looked at her through hard blue eyes. '*He* doesn't care about me; he's hardly looked at me since Lucy was born, and she's been such a difficult baby. I wish I'd never had her.'

'Don't talk rubbish; she's beautiful.'

Juliet shrugged. 'Oh, she looks like an angel, but she's always grizzling. Wakes me up at all hours.'

Miranda was shocked. It sounded so strange coming from Juliet, who revelled in babies. Could she be suffering from postnatal depression? Lucy was four months old, but there had been cases of delayed depression. If she was depressed she needed help. She would ask Tom tomorrow what he thought. Perhaps Juliet could be persuaded to see him professionally.

She put an arm round Juliet's shoulder. 'Come on, love, let's go to bed. It's been a long day. I'll have Lucy in with me and give her her bottle if she wakes in the night to make sure you have a good rest.'

To her surprise, Juliet refused. 'Oh, no, there's no need for that. She'll probably sleep through tonight. I'd rather have her with me.'

Would she refuse if she was really suffering postnatal depression? 'Oh, well, it was just a thought. Let's go up.'

Juliet drained her brandy glass. 'Yes, let's,' she said. 'I'm absolutely bushed.'

The house was blessedly quiet and Miranda was having a solitary coffee when the phone rang the next morning. It was Hugo.

'Miranda. . .about Juliet, what's wrong? There's a garbled message on the answerphone—something about me going away, and not loving her. I just don't understand it. She sounded peculiar. Is she ill? Should I come home? Can I speak to her?' His voice was brittle with anxiety.

Her heart sank. What the hell was she going to say to him?

'Well, not right now, Hugo. She and the children are still asleep; they didn't arrive till late last night. But you're not to worry, she's OK—just missing you and feeling a bit sorry for herself. You know our scatty Juliet. Look, ring later and she'll explain everything.'

'But I can't—not till this evening, about ten your time. I'm on my way to a breakfast meeting and I've got meetings lined up for the rest of the day.' His voice cracked. 'Christ, Miranda, I've just got to get this contract or we're bust. Unless it's an emergency I daren't leave now. I'm about to make a breakthrough. Give her my love and tell her things are looking good. Should have solid news by tonight. If it is, I'll be home like a shot. Goodbye.'

As she put the receiver down Juliet appeared in the sitting-room doorway. 'Was that Hugo?'

Yes, he sends his love and he's going to phone tonight. He says things are going well. He's longing to get home.'

Juliet looked smug. 'Did you tell him that I didn't want to speak to him?'

'No, I told him you were resting.' She glared angrily at her sister. 'Do your own dirty work, Juliet. Don't involve me. Stop playing games. He's not having an affair. He's a smashing guy, and you know it. The trouble is that he's spoilt you rotten and you resent having to take second place to his work for once, though he's doing it for you and the children. Support him, for God's sake.'

Tears welled up in Juliet's blue eyes. 'Well, I never thought you'd turn against me,' she said bitterly. 'I thought you'd understand.'

Miranda softened. 'I think I do, love. You're tired and wanted to make him notice you and the baby. But you see, he's tired too because he's worried and has been working so hard. Let him see that you appreciate that; don't let the loving be all on his side.'

Juliet, looking like a little girl, scrubbed at her eyes

with a tissue. 'But it isn't. It's because I love him so much that I hate him having to work so hard. He tried to tell me things were bad, but I wouldn't believe him and he got so cross and we had an almighty row. And he's not having an affair with his secretary. That was an excuse to run away and give him a fright.'

'Well, you've done that, so now start putting things right. Speak to him tonight; tell him that you love him. Love's so precious, Juliet. If you've got it, hang onto it.'

All the fight had gone out of her. She said quietly, 'I intend to. I've been such a selfish bitch. You're right, love is precious,' and added thoughtfully, 'You're in love with that smashing Dr Brodie, aren't you? He was brilliant last night—very kind, super with the children.'

'I didn't think you noticed, you were so upset.'

'He's difficult not to notice—he's so, well, commanding. I felt safe when he took charge. And you're obviously crackers about each other—that came over loud and clear. I'm glad, Miranda. You've been on your own long enough; a career's fine, but it won't keep you warm at night.'

Miranda said drily, 'So you can recommend marriage and family life, can you?'

Juliet blushed and produced a tremulous smile. 'You can't beat it. It's a great institution.'

The doorbell rang.

'That'll be Tom,' said Miranda.

'Then I'll disappear,' said Juliet, and she fled upstairs.

Miranda opened the door. Tom was standing in the porch, tall, solid, medical bag in hand—every inch a visiting doctor.

His intelligent brown eyes swept over her face.

He smiled. 'Hi,' he said huskily. 'How are things?'

'Surprising,' she murmured, smiling back at him and pressing herself against the wall so that he could squeeze past her into the narrow hall.

His body brushed against hers as he slid past, and she drew in a sharp breath. His mouth quirked at the corners. Children's voices floated down from upstairs.

'Juliet?'

'Up there with the children.'

He steered her into the sitting-room, kicked the door to behind him, put down his bag, gathered her into his arms and crushed her to his broad, tweed-jacketed chest. She could feel the steady thrum of his heart, beating against her soft breasts. He bent his head and bruised her lips with a long, hard kiss and, gently probing, thrust his tongue into the soft moistness of her mouth.

They remained locked together for endless minutes until at last he lifted his head and murmured, 'I needed that,' and then added, 'What do you mean, "surprising"?'

Miranda blinked. 'Oh, the way things have turned out. Hugo phoned, frantic with worry over Juliet who'd left him a crazy mixed-up message. He was torn between rushing back to her or staying to tie up the deal that will keep a roof over their heads. I persuaded him to stay, but I was furious with Juliet and let rip at her. Amazingly, she did a U-turn and admitted she'd invented the story about Hugo being unfaithful.'

'Wanted to give him a short sharp shock; make him notice her?'

'Exactly. How did you know?'

'It happens. Young pretty woman, struggling with three small children, at the end of her tether, tired out, not getting enough help from busy husband. Do almost anything to attract his attention. In your sister's case, perhaps feeling especially vulnerable with a young baby to care for.'

'Last night I thought she might be suffering from

delayed postnatal depression she seemed so bitter about Lucy, but I think that was all part of the act. She does play-act occasionally—has done since she was a little girl—but never over anything serious until now.'

The thought saddened her and it showed in her face.

Tom said gently, 'To get her own way?'

'Yes. But, Tom, don't get the idea that she's selfish. She's warm-hearted and generous, and has always been a wonderful wife and mother until this happened.'

He said firmly, 'And still is. After all, as she saw it, she was fighting for her husband and children; the business was like the other woman. All she needs is to be reassured that Hugo loves her.'

'I think she realises that now, since I made quite a thing of it when I got mad with her. She can't wait for him to ring again tonight. He's promised to come home at once and whisk her back to York when the deal's fixed.'

Tom gave her a lopsided grin that left her breathless. 'So, life could be back to normal for us in a day or two—just the practice to worry about, and the odd epidemic and staff shortages.'

'Fingers crossed, we could be lucky.'

Three days later Juliet, the children and their baggage were loaded into the car, ready to journey back to York. It was soon after dawn. Hugo was spraying the windscreen with de-icer.

Honey-gold, the crenellated towers of the cathedral stood out sharply above the rooftops against the leaden grey sky.

Miranda shivered as she stood on the narrow pavement, waiting to see them off. Well, that was my three days off, she thought wryly, but all's well that ends well, and tonight Tom and I. . .

She hugged her waxed jacket closely round her. It

was bitterly cold; there was a hint of snow in the air.

She bent down to speak to Juliet through the partly open window. 'Take care, love, and have a good journey. Phone directly you arrive; I'll be at the centre till about five,' she reminded for the umpteenth time.

Juliet lowered her window further. 'Stop mothering me like an old hen,' she said with a smile. 'Even slightly jet-lagged, Hugo's a good driver. And, yes, I'll phone.'

Tom and Henry strolled along the terrace and stood beside Miranda. Henry licked her hand and Tom bent to brush her cold cheek with cold lips.

'Morning, my darling.'

'Morning.' They loved each other with their eyes.

Ben and Daisy beamed at Henry, and waved chubby hands. Henry waved his elegant feathery tail in reply. The children fell about laughing.

Juliet smiled shyly at Tom. 'Thanks for everything,' she said simply. 'I must have been a pain, turning up when I did. I'm so happy for you and Miranda. She's always looked after me; make sure you look after her.'

'On my honour,' he promised.

Hugo shook hands with Tom and kissed Miranda. 'Come to us for Christmas,' he invited as he climbed into the driving seat. 'It's going to be the best ever, thanks to you two playing fairy godparents.'

'Sorry, but we'll be too busy,' replied Tom, draping an arm round Miranda's shoulders. 'Patients are no respecters of high days and holidays—they still get sick. I'll probably be on call over much of Christmas.'

'Oh, well, if you find you can manage it the offer's there.'

'Thanks.'

A few flakes of snow fluttered down as Hugo put the car into gear and drove away. Miranda and Tom waved till they were out of sight.

'And what,' asked Miranda, teeth chattering as a

biting wind gusted along the terrace, 'are we going to be so busy doing that made you turn down Hugo's invitation so high-handedly without consulting me?' She tried to sound indignant, but failed. To her utter astonishment, she had enjoyed him making the decision for her.

'Making up for lost time, making love, getting engaged,' replied Tom steadily, as if he were reeling off a list of symptoms. His dark brown eyes were grave behind his horn-rimmed spectacles. 'Planning our wedding. I thought early spring in the cathedral chapel. Perhaps tie the lover's knot on St Valentine's Day, your birthday. What could be more appropriate?'

Her teeth stopped chattering, her jaw dropped open, she gulped in raw cold air and coughed till tears ran down her cheeks.

Gently Tom smoothed away the tears and patted her back. 'All right, my love?'

She stared at him in disbelief, then found a croaky voice. Her eyes glittered greenly. 'No, I'm not all right. I'm furious, dumbfounded, shocked by your arrogance. Arranging my future when you haven't even *asked* me to marry you, never mind find out if I want to. It's unbelievable, incredible.'

'Why?' Tom's voice came out sharp and staccato, his warm breath hanging in the freezing air.

At their feet Henry whimpered and shifted uneasily.

'Because. . .because. . .' She shivered violently.

Tom took her arm, steered her down the brick path to the cottage and pushed her unceremoniously through the door and into the sitting-room.

They stood facing each other on the hearthrug in front of the empty grate, white with the ashes of yesterday's fire.

'Because we haven't jumped into bed together yet,

Miranda, and you don't know how I'll perform—is that it?'

She shook her head violently. 'No,' she whispered, 'of course it isn't.' She had never heard him utter a crudity before.

'Is it because you want a formal proposal, even though you know that we belong to each other come hell or high water, and if Juliet hadn't turned up the other night I would have proposed then?'

Miranda didn't speak; couldn't speak. She just stared at him with wide eyes. . .

'Right, then, that's soon remedied.'

He went down on one knee in front of her, and took her nerveless hands in his. 'My dear, very dear, lovely Miranda, I love you. Will you marry me?' He lifted her hands to his lips and kissed her fingertips.

Time stood still as she looked down at his lean, intelligent, beloved face, and the remnants of her anger fled. He was kind and infinitely gentle as only a strong man could be, as well as arrogant and commanding, and she loved him with every fibre of her being—heart and soul—and had done since the day they'd met. He was the only man for her. And he loved her; he'd said so.

She said simply, because there was nothing else she could or wanted to say, 'Yes, Tom, I'll marry you.'

'Thank you.' He stood up and cupped her face in his hands. 'I'll see that you never regret it,' he murmured. There had been no flowery phrases, yet he'd said all there was to say. He kissed her—not passionately but lightly—on the mouth, sealing their bargain.

The cathedral clock chimed eight.

He checked his watch. 'Damn, I hate to leave you, but I'll have to go or I'll be late for surgery. I'll pick you up around eight-twenty, after I've dropped Henry off, and we'll go in together.'

It was tempting to be a little longer alone in his company before they were thrust into the busy maelstrom of the centre's day, but she shook her head and her lips curved into a smile. 'No, thanks, my darling. I'm going to jog in as usual; get my mind in some sort of order, ponder—there's nothing like jogging to help one ponder.'

He ran his forefinger round her smiling mouth, and his touch was sexy, suggestive. 'What's there to ponder on, dear heart?' he asked softly, but his dark eyes gleamed knowingly.

'You and I, the future, love, happiness, being proposed to,' she breathed.

'You must have had a dozen proposals.'

'But never one at dawn on a cold winter's day, and from the man I love on his knee. . .I want to savour it.'

Her sea-green eyes were brimming with love and laughter. She was absolutely, totally beautiful and desirable. Tom's heart banged away in his broad chest. It took all his considerable self-control to stop himself grabbing her and making mad, savage love to her there and then in front of the dead fireplace.

He groaned and dropped his hands to his sides. 'All right, woman, jog, ponder,' he ground out, 'but we'll have a pub lunch at one, and tonight. . .'

'Tonight, my dearest, is all yours.'

Liz had started her extended weekend leave and Miranda took over her morning general clinic which finished at twelve, leaving her free to concentrate for an hour on admin chores.

She was phoning through an order to their pharmaceutical suppliers when Tom arrived sharp at one.

'Five minutes,' she mouthed when he appeared in the doorway.

He crossed to her desk and, standing behind her,

lifted her thick plait of honey-gold hair and dropped a kiss on her neck.

'Nice,' she mumbled, shivering with sheer wanton pleasure as his lips touched her skin. She tilted her head and smiled up at him, then turned her attention back to the phone. Tom gently kneaded the back of her neck and shoulders and she purred with pleasure.

Sitting close, so that all down one side their shoulders, arms and thighs rubbed sensuously together, they lunched at The Cellary wine bar on Brie, French bread and Perrier water. They made love with their eyes and the occasional touch of their hands, and fed each other morsels of cheese.

They walked back through the cathedral grounds. It was bitterly cold. Little flurries of snowflakes swirled in the north-east wind and settled on the thin layer that already blanketed the grass and trees and the crenellated towers above them.

It was magic. Absorbed in each other, unnoticing of the cold—warmed by their love—they reached the centre and let themselves in at the side door of the building. There was a murmur of voices coming from Reception at the end of the corridor.

Tom carefully flicked a flake of snow from Miranda's hair. 'Daren't kiss you,' he growled. 'Wouldn't be able to stop.'

Miranda's eyes shone like stars. 'We'll make up for it tonight. I'll have a meal ready for eight.'

'We could go to my place. Pinky. . .'

She put a finger to his lips. 'I want to prepare a meal for you. It'll be simple, nothing grand. I'm not the world's greatest cook, but I just want to feed you.'

It was another way of telling him that she loved him.

'It'll be a feast to remember,' he said softly.

* * *

He arrived at the cottage promptly at eight, bearing a bottle of chilled vintage champagne and a box of expensive hand-made chocolates from Annies in the High Street.

'Very grand,' said Miranda, accepting his gifts and desperately trying to subdue the wild beating of her heart when their hands touched. He was here in her cottage and tonight, at last, they were going to make love. 'But I told you it would only be a simple meal. It's mushroom soup, salmon steaks, jacket potatoes and a side salad, with fresh fruit salad and cream to follow.' The words tumbled out.

'Sounds out of this world,' said Tom, peeling off his snow-dusted sheepskin jacket to reveal a heather-coloured cashmere sweater beneath.

He had never looked so strong and masculine. He dominated the tiny hall.

Miranda looked up at him, loving him and wanting to tell him so but not able to find the words. She had waited so long for this moment. She had never properly loved before; hadn't wanted to make love to the men who saw her just as a beautiful ornament.

But she ached to make love to Tom; to give herself to him without holding back. The remnants of her cool, sophisticated reserve crumbled. She felt suddenly shy, a little scared that she wouldn't be able to match his skilful love-making. She lowered her lashes to veil her eyes.

Without a word, Tom took the bottle and box out of her hands and placed them on the narrow side-table.

'Don't be frightened, dear heart,' he murmured.

Very gently he cradled her upturned face in his hands and kissed her closed lids, her nose and cheeks and the slender column of her throat and then traced round her lips with the tip of his tongue.

She sighed against his mouth and he pulled her

closer, dropping his hands from her face and sliding them down the shimmering silk of her dress—running his fingers down the length of her spine until they moulded themselves over the firm curve of her buttocks. He pressed her even closer, their bodies melting into each other.

Her arms were round his neck, her fingers tangled in his hair. His body was hard against her softness. She could feel his erection, strong and pulsing.

'Love me,' she whispered.

He scooped her up in his arms, carried her into the sitting-room and lowered her with great care onto the sofa bed opposite the fireplace. The dead ashes of the morning were gone; pine logs blazed and spluttered in the elegant steel grate. Candles in silver candlesticks burnt steadily on the polished table at the end of the room.

The sapphire-blue curtains, which matched Miranda's dress, were drawn across the casement windows.

'You're sure about this, my love?' he asked.

'I've never been more sure of anything in my life,' said Miranda.

They undressed slowly—helping each other with buttons and zips—until at last they were naked on the sofa, facing each other and bathed in the orange-red glow of the fire.

'Your skin is like golden satin,' whispered Tom, levering himself up onto one elbow to look down on her.

His eyes, dark and sultry, caressed her. He brushed his lips across her slim, rounded shoulders and down to the yielding mounds of her breasts, which he kissed reverently, circling their softness—nibbling hungrily with teeth and tongue and lips at her nipples until they grew rosily erect.

Her breasts felt full to bursting, and she cried out softly with the sheer pain and pleasure of the sensation.

Tom raised his head at once. 'Are you all right, dear heart?' His voice was low, husky.

'Oh, yes, yes,' she breathed.

She wrapped her arms round his lean, muscular torso and held him close, rubbing her smooth, tender breasts slowly and sensuously against the wiry hairiness of his broad chest. Her nipples against his nipples.

She said breathlessly, 'Love me, please love me.'

Carefully he rolled over on top of her and, nudging apart her legs with strong thighs, gradually, with little thrusting movements, eased himself into her warm, receptive, innermost self.

With savage tenderness he thrust and receded, adapting his rhythm to hers, until at last they reached their peak and climaxed together. Wave after wave of shuddering, ecstatic joy washed over them as, crooning and murmuring, they clung together quivering and sweating.

At last the fierce, pulsating ecstasy began to subside and Tom, still staying with her and cradling her in his arms, rolled onto his side. He kissed her gently, and stroked a few errant strands of honey-gold hair back from her flushed face.

'Thank you; that was some loving,' he said simply. 'And for you, dear heart?'

Miranda gave him a radiant smile. 'You've melted the ice,' she said softly. 'I didn't know it could be like that. I feel utterly content, fulfilled, a complete woman, no hang-ups for the first time ever.' Her luminous sea-green eyes met his. 'I do love you,' she murmured, 'so very much.'

They were married on St Valentine's Day, Miranda's birthday, just as Tom had planned.

The Lady Mary chapel in the cathedral was filled with expensive early spring flowers—daffodils, tulips, narcissi, mimosa—a gift from Dr Withers who was making a slow but steady recovery from his stroke.

'But I want to do it, my dear,' he'd said gruffly when Miranda had protested at his generosity. 'You've made Tom happy, and that makes me happy. You're good for him, and you're good for the practice. Not,' he'd added, with a surprising twinkle in his eyes, 'that you must let that interfere with any future plans you may have in mind.'

He had grinned roguishly and said with something of his former pithiness, 'What I'm saying is ditch the practice if you want to start a family; don't sacrifice yourself to it. A family is what Tom needs, and I wouldn't be averse to a few proxy grandchildren.' And then he'd apologised. 'Impertinent, that; you must ignore a sentimental old man. Just be happy, my dear.'

And Miranda radiated beauty and happiness as she sailed up the aisle on her wedding day on Hugo's arm, followed by a solemn five-year-old Daisy in rose taffeta and carrying a posy of anemones.

Her wedding dress was classically simple. Flaring at the ankle, the soft, oyster-coloured silk—with a scooped-out neckline and long sleeves—moulded itself to her slender figure. Her honey-blonde hair was plaited into a regal coronet, topped by a scrap of lace held in place by a ring of silk flowers.

She carried a sheath of feathery fern, sweet-scented jonquil and purple irises.

Tom, with Val beside him—both distinguished in grey morning suits—turned to look at her with loving and admiring eyes as she took her place at his side.

Blushing with pleasure, Miranda smiled at him serenely.

Little Daisy, composed and well briefed as to what

she was to do, stepped forward to take Miranda's bouquet.

The congregation was suddenly quiet; the service began.

'Dearly beloved. . .'

Tom took her right hand into his as the beautiful words of the ancient ceremony flowed about them. She was glad that they'd chosen the old-style marriage service.

'With this ring. . .'

Slowly, reverently, Tom slipped the plain, wide gold band onto her wedding finger.

'You may kiss the bride. . .'

It was over; they were married. In a dream, they signed the register. They were now officially man and wife—Dr and Mrs Thomas Brodie.

A joyful peal of bells rang out as they stood on the porch. Cameras and camcorders whirred and clicked.

The crowd of people waiting outside was dominated by women with small children—dozens of them.

'Good Lord,' exclaimed Tom in astonishment, 'it's the mother and toddler clinic. What on earth are they doing here?'

Miranda was less astonished. 'I think they've come to wish us well,' she said. 'They've been asking me for weeks what time we were getting married.'

'No one asked me,' he said.

'They probably felt shy about asking you something so personal. Nurses are easier to approach,' she explained. 'We're good go-betweens.'

A small Down's syndrome boy—a regular visitor to the clinic—toddled up to them clutching a silver cardboard horseshoe on a satin ribbon, but was uncertain what to do with it.

Tom bent down and lifted the child up. 'Jamie, let's

give it to Sister,' he suggested gently.

Jamie thrust the horseshoe at Miranda and, leaning forward, planted a wet kiss on her cheek, then wriggled to the ground and trotted back to his mother.

Miranda said softly, 'I'm so proud of you—you're so super with these little ones.'

His eyes gleamed. 'Well, my nurse is the world's best go-between,' he murmured.

The photographer called everyone to order. 'Now a special for the album—bride and groom, family and close friends.'

This is the one that I shall cherish, thought Miranda, glancing round the group assembled on the cathedral steps.

They were short on relatives—only Juliet, Hugo and the children, and on Tom's side an elderly aunt—but big on close friends. Val, of course, Dr Withers in a wheelchair, the senior practice doctors—Bill, Kay, Lydia and Stella—and Pat and Liz, and Sue and Andrew Palmer and the Pinks.

'Some day,' muttered Tom, squeezing Miranda's hand, 'we'll have to do something about this family shortfall.'

Miranda's eyes sparkled. 'What a lovely idea,' she said huskily. 'Why didn't I think of that?'

'Oh, you'd have got around to it,' said Tom.

'Smile please,' said the photographer, and everyone smiled.

COMING NEXT MONTH

THE PERFECT WIFE AND MOTHER?
by Caroline Anderson

Audley Memorial Hospital

Ryan O'Connor wanted a lover. No commitment, no ties. And Ginny Jeffries agreed, against her better judgement, to accept Ryan O'Connor's terms. But being his lover meant deepening ties with Ryan and his two small children, and all she could see ahead was heartbreak...

INTIMATE PRESCRIPTION by Margaret Barker

Adam Lennox was surprised to see that Trisha Redman was a mother. Eight years previously she had refused to marry him because she was fearful of a physical relationship. So how could she enjoy a physical relationship with another man? Would Trisha tell Adam the truth?

PROMISE OF A MIRACLE by Marion Lennox

Gundowring Hospital

Meg Preston's quiet visit to Gundowring took an unexpected turn when she fell into the path—and home—of Rob Daniels. Before she knew it she was bound up in the Gundowring way of life and was falling in love with Rob! But Meg had a fiancé waiting in England...

WINNING THROUGH by Laura MacDonald

Dr Harry Brolin forecast that Kirstin Patterson would only survive one month as a GP in his tough inner city practice. She soon proved that she could handle even the most perilous of situations. But could she handle her dangerous feelings for Harry?

Available from WH Smith, John Menzies, Volume One, Forbuoys, Martins, Woolworths, Tesco, Asda, Safeway and other paperback stockists.

How would you like to win a year's supply of Mills & Boon® books? Well you can and they're FREE! Simply complete the competition below and send it to us by 31st December 1997. The first five correct entries picked after the closing date will each win a year's subscription to the Mills & Boon series of their choice. What could be easier?

SPADE
SUNSHINE
PICNIC
BEACHBALL
SWIMMING
SUNBATHING
CLOUDLESS
FUN
TOWEL
SAND
HOLIDAY

W	Q	T	U	H	S	P	A	D	E	M	B
E	Q	R	U	O	T	T	K	I	U	I	E
N	B	G	H	L	H	G	O	D	W	K	A
I	I	O	A	I	N	E	S	W	Q	L	C
H	N	U	N	D	D	F	W	P	E	O	H
S	U	N	B	A	T	H	I	N	G	L	B
N	S	E	A	Y	F	C	M	D	A	R	A
U	B	P	K	A	N	D	M	N	U	T	L
S	E	N	L	I	Y	B	I	A	N	U	L
H	B	U	C	K	E	T	N	S	N	U	E
T	A	E	W	T	O	H	G	H	O	T	F
C	L	O	U	D	L	E	S	S	P	W	N

C7F

Please turn over for details of how to enter ☞

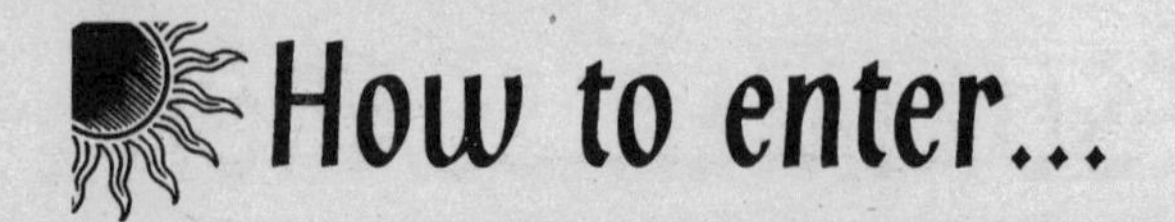

How to enter...

Hidden in the grid are eleven different summer related words. You'll find the list beside the word puzzle overleaf and they can be read backwards, forwards, up, down and diagonally. As you find each word, circle it or put a line through it. When you have found all eleven, don't forget to fill in your name and address in the space provided below and pop this page in an envelope (you don't even need a stamp) and post it today. Hurry competition ends 31st December 1997.

Mills & Boon Summer Search Competition
FREEPOST, Croydon, Surrey, CR9 3WZ
EIRE readers send competition to PO Box 4546, Dublin 24.

Please tick the series you would like to receive if you are a winner
Presents™ ❑ Enchanted™ ❑ Temptation® ❑
Medical Romance™ ❑ Historical Romance™ ❑

Are you a Reader Service™ Subscriber? Yes ❑ No ❑

Ms/Mrs/Miss/Mr ______________________________
(BLOCK CAPS PLEASE)

Address ______________________________

____

______________________ Postcode ______________________

(I am over 18 years of age)

One application per household. Competition open to residents of the UK and Ireland only.
You may be mailed with other offers from other reputable companies as a result of this application. If you would prefer not to receive such offers, please tick box. ❑

C7F